6 Dates
to Disaster

by Cynthia T. Toney

Write Integrity
Press

6 Dates to Disaster

ISBN-10: 1-944120-24-6
ISBN-13: 978-1-944120-24-5
E-Book ISBN: 978-1-944120-23-8

Published by:
 Write Integrity Press
 PO Box 702852
 Dallas, TX 75370

Contact the author at birdfacewendy@gmail.com or
www.cynthiattoney.com
www.WriteIntegrity.com
Printed in the United States of America.

Praise for
6 DATES TO DISASTER
and the Bird Face series:

6 Dates to Disaster shows us the world of a teenage girl in her first year of high school, complete with romance, disappointment, determination and the tendency toward self-centered motivation intertwined with genuine regard for others. I especially loved the flea-market jewelry box that provides a touching end to a story I recommend without reservation.

~Mary L. Hamilton, author of the *Rustic Knoll Bible Camp Series*

In Books 1 and 2 of the Bird Face series, the struggles of Wendy Robichaud through her early teens were both entertaining and encouraging. With humor, wit, common sense and faith, Cynthia Toney keeps readers glued to the pages. Now in Book 3, another mysterious note kicks off Wendy's next journey into adolescent friendships and a collision with humility, forgiveness and generosity.

~Glenn Haggerty, author of *Run* (Intense Series)

Cynthia T. Toney's Bird Face series captures the young teenage years well. Toney weaves serious issues in with humor, mystery, and interesting storylines, making these books hard to put down. The challenges and surprises faced by the characters, especially Wendy Robichaud, help them grow and also bring to light issues relevant to today's teens.

~Theresa Linden, author of *Battle for His Soul, Life-Changing Love,* and *Roland West, Loner.*

Cynthia T. Toney knows how to spin a yarn. I enjoyed *8 Notes to a Nobody* and *10 Steps to Girlfriend Status.* Now with book three, *6 Dates to Disaster*, Wendy faces life's challenges on the more adult level. Ms. Toney is never guilty of author intrusion, weaving tales with spot on pace and intrigue.

~Jean Ann Williams, author of *Just Claire* (Clean Reads)

… most emotionally moving … it's never easy to see someone you love lose their grip on life. Cynthia Toney does a lovely job handling this difficult topic [in *10 Steps to Girlfriend Status*]."

~A.J. Cattapan, author of
Angelhood and *Seven Riddles to Nowhere*

Dedication

To honesty
and hard work.

Acknowledgements

Even more than the two previous books of this series, God assisted me in writing *6 Dates to Disaster*. I didn't know where to start until He placed the image in my head of—well, I can't tell you, in case you're reading these acknowledgements before you read the story.

I appreciate very much the friends and other readers who told me which characters they enjoyed in the first two books. That helped me make a number of decisions.

Huge thanks go to my beta readers for the speed with which they provided feedback. One special young reader shared precisely what she hoped to see in the next book. I'll be happy to oblige!

It's a wonderful feeling to know that my publisher and my editor make sure even the small stuff is as good as it can be. By the time a book is about to release, I'm cross-eyed!

For everyone who has purchased, reviewed, or shared information about any of my books, I am forever grateful.

And for listening no matter what, I thank my husband.

Chapter 1

People will hide just about anything inside a jewelry box—especially a secret.

As a kid, I tried saving a hard-boiled Easter egg in mine. But during a warm Louisiana spring, it doesn't take long for that secret to get out.

Two hours on a Saturday afternoon at the biggest flea market in the parish, and I hadn't found a single jewelry box.

My stepsister, Alice, and I hoofed from table to table, covering territory as quickly as possible. Wearing shorts … in February.

If it hadn't been for the merchants' canopies, we would've sunburned. A little more air between my body and the one standing next to me would've been nice, but the place was too crowded with shoppers.

"How adorable!" A lady at the next booth squealed over a wooden Easter bunny yard ornament that could be personalized with her child's name.

I crossed my eyes. Even as a six-year-old, I wouldn't have wanted anything in front of my house to read "Wendy."

Enough distractions. Back to the day's goal. Finding a jewelry box for Mom among thousands of items scattered across a hundred folding tables might be harder than I thought.

"There's too much junk in this flea market." I rolled my shoulders and sighed.

The booth owner stared daggers at me.

"Haven't you spent enough time looking? Why don't you just buy her a new one?" Alice flicked perspiration from above her lip with a fingertip. Her strawberry-blonde hair had begun to frizz, and she lifted it off her neck, fanning it behind her.

I shook my head, ponytail slapping my jaw. "Anyone can go to a store and do that. It'll mean more to Mom if the jewelry box has history—or at least some character. I know the right one is here somewhere."

Alice shrugged. "You should know. She's been your mom longer than she's been mine." She picked up a dingy-white crocheted vest and held it against her front.

Mom and Papa D—short for Daniel—had been married almost six months. In the four months between the end of eighth grade and my first semester at LeMoyne High School, Alice had gone from being a classmate I hardly knew to being both my running buddy and my sister. We suffered through our share of quarrels, but living with each other had become easier since Christmas. And it was nice having a sister to go with me on errands. If only she would focus.

Alice sniffed the vest under the armholes. She slid her hands through the openings and shrugged the vest onto her shoulders.

My gaze traveled two booths down toward a collection of antique-looking tabletop accessories. "I'll be over there." I pointed.

"I'm coming." Alice slipped out of the garment and followed me.

Rusted and tarnished items cluttered the table. A pair of wrought-iron candlesticks towered above the rest of the display.

I gasped. Beneath the candlesticks sat a large

mahogany box almost the same color as our hair—Mom's and mine.

Hands shaking, I moved the candlesticks aside and lifted the box. It contained three drawers with brass pulls. The sides and hinged top showed only a few scratches. I set the box back down and opened one of the drawers.

"See?" I whispered as though in the presence of a holy relic. "This is what I'm talking about." I glanced at Alice to make sure she was paying attention. "Made of solid wood with red velvet inside. You can even see impressions in the velvet where bangle bracelets were stored. This is all *real*."

Alice rolled her blue eyes but grinned.

"It's the right size, too—much bigger than her old one. It should hold all her jewelry and Grand-mère Robichaud's antique pieces. She won't need those cardboard boxes anymore. She'll love it."

"Then let's get it." Alice reached inside her pocket for some money, which she'd never lacked since I'd known her. As part of the Rend family, Mom and I were still getting used to having extra money for luxury items.

Alice and I split the cost fifty-fifty, and I bagged the box. I'd never spent that much on a gift before, but Mom was worth it.

Alice phoned Papa D that we'd meet him and my little stepbrother, Adam, at the car. They'd found gifts for Mom, too.

This was going to be her best birthday ever.

Papa D stopped his car in the driveway so I could get out and check the mail. I rifled through the stack as I made my way to the house.

I halted, my athletic shoes screeching on the cement.

A letter from Anchorage, Alaska! Nice and thick, too. I pushed forward.

Please, God, let it hold good news from Sam about Mrs. V.

Or at least not bad news that her Alzheimer's had worsened.

Mrs. Villaturo had been gone how long now? Five months, but she was the only grandmother I had, even though she was really Sam's. I'd accepted the fact that Mrs. V had to move close to her family so they could look out for her. But after living next door to her at my old house and seeing her every day for eight years, I worried how she was doing and when I'd ever see her again.

I dumped the rest of the mail on the foyer table. Dashing in a zigzag obstacle course around our dogs, Belle and Chanceaux, I headed to my room.

The bag holding the jewelry box sat on the floor inside my door where Alice must've placed it. I passed it and crossed the room. With the envelope from Alaska tucked under my chin, I opened a window to let the heat escape. *Good, a breeze.* I switched on the ceiling fan to clear the remaining hot air.

My chest tightened as I inserted a finger under the flap and ripped it open. The pages unfolded to Sam's big, blocky print. I giggled with my mouth closed. He shouted when he wrote—and he was the deaf one. My chest loosened.

Hi, Wendy.

How are you?

No bad news to start, thank goodness. I plopped on the edge of my bed to read.

Stuff about Christmas and winter vacation. And snow. Sam and his buddies from the deaf school were still having snowball fights. And here I was, sweating.

If only I could be there. I closed my eyes and imagined luminous, cooling crystals sprinkling onto my skin like fairy's magic. I inhaled deeply through my nose and felt the frigid air biting inside my nostrils. For a moment, I played in the snow with Sam, smashing a snowball in his face, his eyes glowing warm.

Silly daydreaming. I blinked hard and returned to the words on the page.

A snowplow had to clear the road for my dad and me to visit Grandma at the assisted-living home yesterday.

A jealous pang struck my heart. At least Sam and his dad, Tony, got to spend time with her. Tony—not my favorite person—wouldn't listen when I tried to help Mrs. V stay in Louisiana so I could visit her. But although I couldn't see her myself, I was happy for Mrs. V that Sam and his family lived near her new home. I'd talked to her twice on the phone since she left, when Sam thought she was having a good day. She'd received my Christmas card and thanked me for it, her voice light and sweet. I'd almost cried.

The second page was one of Sam's pencil sketches—an original, not a copy. He'd drawn a scene through his bedroom window. Wow, so this was what it looked like outside his house, the snow disguising everything but the trees. I'd seen snow only twice that I could remember. Its thin layer on the ground hadn't lasted but a day or two. No comparison to the billowy mounds of white depicted in

Sam's drawing.

I moved to the next page, and a note fell onto my lap.

From Mrs. V! She'd used elegant ivory stationery with a black monogrammed "V" at the top. Her script ran uneven and broken like that of a child learning to write. But she must've been clear-headed. She described her apartment, the courtyard view, and the friendly people she'd met who took care of her.

My worry eased, knowing they treated her kindly.

I miss you, Wendy, and I hope you'll be able to come see me soon.

My eyes filled with tears, my heart aching for a talk with her in person. I lowered the note to my knee, sniffed, and blinked.

The charcoal portrait Sam had done of Mrs. V and me before they left in September hung on the wall opposite my bed. I'd spent a month's allowance to buy the frame it deserved. It was the most beautiful remembrance Sam could've given me. But sometimes it hurt to look at the picture, I missed her so much. I wiped the corners of my eyes with a knuckle.

And I missed Sam, too. I wasn't often willing to admit it, even to myself, but I thought about him a lot. He acted as much a friend to me as people I'd known for years—

after I got used to him. Once I adjusted to the way his voice sounded all nasally and harsh because of his deafness and focused on his eyes and his body language, he communicated kindness and caring better than most hearing people.

I sighed. Well, enough of that sappy stuff. At least Mrs. V was doing fine for now. I set her note aside and continued with Sam's letter.

Keep working on your parents to let you visit us. Mom and my sister, Sarah, already have the guest room prepared so you and Alice can spend a couple days here if you like. They made me get all my sports equipment out, so I hope I didn't waste my time.

I snorted. Guys. The same everywhere.

If you plan to stay at least two weeks during the summer, I can get you on as a short-term volunteer with Alaska Wildlife Conservation. We'd have a great time together.

I was working on getting there, every chance I got. Mom said we might take a family vacation to Anchorage in June or July. Summers were beautiful and cool. If Mrs. V could hold on in spite of the Alzheimer's …

My stomach flipped, and I gave my head a quick shake. *No.* No sad thoughts today. Mom's birthday was

Friday, and we finally had a family to celebrate with us.

I finished Sam's letter, my spirits lifting by his funny story of a deaf basketball game. Two players had an argument in sign language, some of it not very nice. Sam knew how to make me laugh and feel comfortable about being able to hear when he couldn't.

Learn enough American Sign Language before you come to Alaska so these jerks I call friends can't talk about you right in front of your face. LOL.

Later,

Sam

P.S. I know you can do it.

I took a deep breath, puffed my cheeks, and blew it out. The book on ASL I'd checked out of the library—and renewed twice—rested on the shelf of my nightstand. My finger movements in mimicking the photographs to form the letters were awkward, spastic-looking. I'd tried watching videos online, but the instructors' fingers moved so fast, I couldn't follow them. After pausing the video a hundred times, I'd given up.

The alphabet would take a lot of practice to spell even my own name smoothly, and I still had a bunch of the most common whole-word signs to memorize. I reached for the book and placed it on the bed next to me. I'd better try again tonight.

I folded Mrs. V's note with Sam's letter and returned them both to the envelope to answer later. I had other things to do.

The jewelry box needed a closer visual inspection than I'd given it at the flea market. If it needed some serious TLC, I'd better get started.

I carried the bag holding the jewelry box into the window's natural light and withdrew the box. Tilting it one way and another, I examined the wood surfaces.

Humph. Next to all the other grimy antiques on the booth's display table, it hadn't seemed that dirty. I set the box down and headed to the bathroom.

I grabbed an old washcloth and dampened it under the faucet. Sitting cross-legged on the floor under the window, I wiped the outside of the box clean.

The insides of the drawers contained some grunge and small amounts of trash. One at a time, I slid each drawer out and dumped its contents onto the floor. A paper clip, a few buttons, an earring back. Real gold? I held it up to the light. *Nah.*

So many scraps of paper. Wadded department store receipts. Half a business card from an eye doctor.

A tightly folded piece of blue paper was stuck in the

back corner of a drawer. I pulled it free and unfolded the bottom of a page from one of those small-sized spiral notebooks people use for journals. It had one edge of ragged paper fingers torn from the spiral, but the paper felt crisp and looked clean. Where had I seen paper like that before? I opened it.

Meet me in the park after the Mardi Gras parade. It was written in a loose, flowing script that could belong to a male or female. No signature. How odd.

My back straightened.

Someone had hidden this note. Hidden it where no one else would find it, shoving it like that to the rear corner of a drawer so small. To keep the meeting a secret without throwing away the note—and still be able to look at it again later. Or, maybe the note never arrived where it was supposed to go.

My curiosity kicked in like it had when I'd learned about a lost uncle no one in the family wanted to talk about.

Who'd written this note, and where was the person it belonged to? One thing for sure—the sender must be someone important to the recipient.

My eyes narrowed. Was the note a directive for a romantic rendezvous? An exchange of some sort? What? How did an old jewelry box wind up at the flea market with what appeared to be a new note still inside?

If the message referred to this year's Mardi Gras parade, it was scheduled for next Saturday.

Anticipation drummed in my chest.

What if the sender or the recipient showed up at the park next Saturday and no one else came?

I threw away everything from inside the box but kept the note.

"Don't fill up on snacks. I'm ordering pizza in a minute." At the kitchen sink, Mom yanked a paper towel from the roll, wet it, and attacked a white paint smudge on her hand.

I lowered a chocolate chip cookie from my lips. "What's the occasion? Besides you being in the middle of a salvage project, of course." A pair of nightstands being painted in the garage awaited new life in the master bedroom.

"Family meeting." Mom scrubbed harder without looking up. "Then we'll watch a movie together. You girls can choose."

Alice chomped a bite of apple and headed toward the

living room. "I'll go see what's available."

Mom dried her hands and reached for a pizza coupon. Thriftiness was a hard habit to break.

The phone in my pocket vibrated, and as I looked at the screen, so did my heart. *David Griffin.* Our relationship stood on solid ground again after dating once in September, breaking up over my friendship with Sam, and then agreeing to start over as friends ourselves. Friends who didn't tell each other who else they could be friends with. Friends who respected what the other person cared about.

We'd finally gone out on another date last weekend to a movie with David's older brother and his girlfriend.

"Just one cookie." I kissed Mom's cheek.

"Hi, David." I carried the cookie and the call to my room.

Life was good.

"How was the flea market?" David's deep, masculine voice made words like *flea* and *market* sound exciting. And he'd just turned fifteen.

"Good. Mission accomplished." My voice strayed toward girly and giddy around him if I wasn't careful. I cleared my throat.

"What did you find?"

"A vintage jewelry box for my mom's birthday next

week."

"Great. Well, if you're not busy next Saturday, maybe you could go with my family and me to the parade. My grandfather commands one of the floats for the army veterans, so we never miss it."

Hearing the word *parade* right after reading the note made my scalp tingle. I rubbed the back of my head. Maybe I could squeeze in some snoop—uh, observing. And it wouldn't be obvious if I were with someone else.

"Yeah. Sure. I'd love to. Just let me clear it with Mom and Papa D." And make sure this outing wouldn't ruin my going with David on an evening date the Saturday after that. In spite of Mom and Papa D's date-only-every-other-weekend rule, going to the parade would be a family event with David's parents. It was a family-friendly Mardi Gras parade, after all. They probably wouldn't count it as a regular date.

"Okay. I hope they let you."

"Me too. What time would you pick me up?"

"Quarter to twelve so we can find a good spot. Parade starts at one. And we should be back by five, my dad said."

"Good, I'll need to tell them that."

"Call me back?"

"I will, after dinner. We're eating soon."

"All right. Later, then. 'Bye, Wendy."

"'Bye, David."

What a successful weekend this was turning out to be.

When the pizza arrived, I'd already gotten permission to go with David to the parade. My family filtered into the kitchen one at a time, grabbed a drink and a paper plate, and took a seat in the dining room. Alice appeared last at the table, eyes red and cheeks flushed.

Uh-oh. What did I miss? She avoided looking my way by staring at her plate. I searched everyone else's faces but got nothing.

Mom sealed her lips together tight.

Papa D cleared his throat, and Alice looked up. "We need to talk as a family about a change that will affect us all, at least for a few months, maybe longer. But it's not a tragedy." He glared at Alice.

She shifted her gaze from his face toward the pizza box.

Adam stared at the box, too, but hungrily. He swung his leg repeatedly and kicked my chair.

"What is it, Papa D?" I reached under the table and

stilled Adam's foot. Whatever Mom and Papa D wanted to talk over with us might not be a tragedy, but I didn't like being the last one to know about anything.

He took a deep breath and spoke without any emotion in his voice. "I was laid off from my job."

"Laid off?" I wouldn't have guessed that. "But 'laid off' means it's temporary, right?"

"No. The company's downsizing, so it's permanent." His jaw clenched.

"Oh." I slumped into my chair. "I'm sorry, Papa D."

Mom stroked my ponytail. "The timing is bad because we just bought this house and have a big mortgage payment now."

Papa D nodded, not making eye contact with anyone, his lips pressed together.

Mom's eyes softened, and she placed her hand over his. "Our budget needed Daniel's income from his job as well as his Air Force retirement to provide for our family. We'd agreed I'd stop working, but now I'll also have to look for a job while he looks for a new one."

"But you'll find another good job, won't you?" I shifted my gaze back and forth between my parents' faces.

"We don't know what we'll find …" Papa D said.

"Or who will find one first," Mom added softly.

"If I were old enough, I'd get a job and help out." I'd have said anything to lift the gloomy cloud hovering over the table. Mom's face had lost its color. Alice's blotchy complexion and downturned mouth weren't helping to lighten anyone's spirits. Adam's head rested on the table like he'd given up on eating any pizza.

Papa D smiled a weak little smile.

My eyes opened wide, and I sat up tall. "I can at least babysit. Maybe every day after school. I could make a ton of money." Not really, but I used a cheerful tone.

Mom's eyelids crinkled at the corners. "You may be able to babysit for someone else once in a while, but if Daniel and I are both away from home a lot, we'll be counting on you and Alice to take care of Adam and do more around the house, too. And of course, your schoolwork."

Alice remained clammed up. It wasn't like her not to offer her two cents in a family discussion. Other than the obvious, what was eating her? There must be more to this than Mom and Papa D were telling.

"What happens if one of you doesn't find a job right away or it doesn't pay enough?"

Papa D swallowed hard. "I'll be honest. That could be the case."

"So what would happen?" No new clothes for Easter? No more pizza? And a realization yanked me so hard my heart skipped a beat. I turned from Papa D to Mom. "What about our vacation to Alaska this summer?"

She shook her head gently. "I'm afraid we can't answer that question right now."

My stomach wrenched. "You mean we're going to have to give up everything we want?"

Everyone else's head jerked in my direction.

Two vertical lines appeared between Mom's eyebrows. "I promise you won't have to make any more sacrifices than anyone else will." As if in pain, she blinked rapidly and swallowed hard.

Her face softened my heart. I'd seen that look before when money was tight after Dad left. She'd worked long hours until she married Papa D and had been so happy staying home the past few months. She loved having time to cook dinner every night and create beautiful things for our new house out of salvaged junk.

Papa D squeezed Mom's hand but spoke to me. "We'll talk more about this another time. Right now, let's give thanks for the food we're about to eat."

I bowed my head and added a silent prayer that I'd find a way to see Mrs. V while she was still alive. And Sam, before he had time to forget me.

It was the quietest pizza dinner we'd ever eaten. No one mentioned watching the movie.

After dinner, Alice and I trudged to our separate rooms. She slammed her door.

I took a deep breath as I phoned David to tell him the parade for next Saturday was on.

He chuckled. "You don't sound very happy about it."

I lifted the pitch of my voice. "Sorry. I am, really. Happy, that is." My stepfather losing his job wasn't the kind of news I wanted to share with anyone. Not yet anyway. Not even with David.

"Are you sure nothing's wrong?"

"Everything's fine." Just a tiny fib. "I'll be ready at eleven forty-five."

"Great. We tailgate out the back of Dad's SUV. My mom will have stuff for us to eat."

"Should I bring a lawn chair?"

"No, we have plenty of those. But you'll have to carry a flag."

"What?"

"A little American flag. You know, to wave high in the air when my grandfather's float goes by. Veterans, remember? We want him to notice us."

"Um, I'm fresh out of flags."

He chuckled again. "Don't worry. I'll have one for you."

"What a relief. I thought for a minute I wouldn't qualify to go." My delivery was dry.

His laughter boomed.

Warmth filled me to the tips of my fingers and toes. He always got it when I tried to be funny. Not everyone did.

"It'll be fun." His voice lowered. "Can't wait to see you."

"Me too." Even though we'd see each other at school all week.

Another male voice came through from the background, followed by grunts and what sounded like a slap. Someone yelled, "Hey!"

"Sorry, Wendy, but I've gotta cut it short. My mom's making my brother and me do our own laundry. Something about not wanting to raise helpless men. I want to beat Ben to the washing machine. I'll see you Monday, okay?"

I laughed. "Okay. Hope you win. 'Bye, David."

"'Bye, Wendy."

I sighed and plugged the phone into its charger.

If only Alice and I could become like David and his brother, playing and teasing each other all the time. Sometimes even their parents joined in, and everybody laughed and had fun. But they'd been together since forever. How long would it take for Alice and me and the rest of our family to be like theirs?

At least I could get out of the house next weekend and be with a family that didn't have so many problems.

A buzzer went off in my brain. *Right*. Being in this new family did feel like one problem after another.

I rubbed my temples. The day had caught up with me, and I blinked heavy lids, my eyeballs dry and scratchy. The temptation to shower and crawl into bed with a book and forget about real life was strong, but I needed to check on Alice. She would do the same for me in spite of any disagreements we'd had. I left my room and rapped lightly on her door.

"Come in."

"Hey, you wanna talk?" I kept my voice low and eased the door closed behind me.

She sat in bed, her back resting on pillows piled high against the headboard, her muscular legs stretched out in front. "If you want." She let the TV remote slip from her hand.

I perched on the edge of the bed. "I'm guessing you already knew about Papa D losing his job." I twisted my mouth to one side.

"Yeah, but only a few minutes before you did." She crossed her arms. "I had asked him for something special, and I sort of dragged it out of him why he couldn't grant it."

"Oh." I studied her face, trying to get a clue to what it could be. "What did you want?"

"Summer music camp at Baylor University." She paused. "That's in Texas."

Texas? I hesitated a sec. "Why not something closer to home?"

Alice's face clouded. "You want to go to Alaska."

My stomach took a roller-coaster plummet. "But that's to see Mrs. V, who's been like a grandmother to me. I hardly remember my grand-mère . She died when I was six years old." I touched my throat, reaching for the gold crucifix she left me, more often around my neck than not.

Alice rolled her eyes. "Yeah, that's the reason."

How mean! I jumped to my feet and placed my hands on my hips. "So what if I get to see Sam, too? Our whole family was going to Alaska for vacation. You'd get to enjoy it as much as I would." My head pounded.

"Well, I need to go to a good music camp every summer so I can improve my clarinet. A prestigious camp where someone who can offer me a scholarship to a top music school will eventually hear me. That's more important than some stupid vacation thousands of miles away." She bugged out her eyes.

My face heated like I'd eaten Tabasco sauce. She didn't have to call the trip stupid. What was she, eight?

I counted to ten and let my anger go for the sake of our friendship and family tie. "I'm just saying that if you choose a camp in Louisiana this time, maybe you can stay with one of my relatives on my Dad's side." My words came out calm and low. "That would save money, and at least you'd get to go to camp."

"You don't understand how important the right camp is." Tears springing to her eyes, she turned away and slid off the opposite side of the bed.

Groan. I did understand how important her music was to her. I really did. It had been her constant friend when she didn't have any other because her military family moved so much.

Her shoulders shook with each sob.

I'd never seen her so upset, not even when I started dating David before she paired up with my cousin Jerome.

She wiped her face with her hands and sniffed.

"Alice, come on. I'm only trying to help." I pleaded with her. "Besides, if it's a music camp close to Bayou Calmon, maybe you could see Jerome more often."

With her back to me, she tossed her hair and tucked her fists under her arms. She was done talking.

I sighed and bit my lip. No use saying anything else and ticking her off further. I slipped out of the room.

One by one, my family's plans were falling apart. There had to be a way to make some money so none of us, including me, had to give up on our dreams. But it had to be bigger money than babysitting would get me.

At church Sunday, Mom knelt for fifteen minutes before Mass started, forehead pressed to her clasped hands. Papa D did that thing guys do when they're thinking— resting elbows on knees while he sat. Maybe Lutherans didn't kneel as much as Catholics did. But he hung his head and closed his eyes, and I could tell he was praying.

I cut my eyes to each side to check if anyone was

watching us. Was it my imagination, or were people looking our way and whispering? Who could possibly know already that Papa D had lost his job? Just the same, I knelt for the second time, close to him, and shielded him from prying eyes.

Chapter 2

The school week was pretty normal, a.k.a. drudgery, except for how quiet my family had become before and after school. Seeing David every now and then during the day added some sparkle, at least. And being with my friend Gayle did, too.

Thursday, at the end of one of our classes together, I caught her staring at me with her cocoa-bean eyes.

"What are you looking all soulful about?" I could say that without it sounding like a racist remark. How could it be? After investigating the disappearance of my great-uncle Andre last fall, I'd discovered Gayle's great-grandmother had secretly married him before he died, and she later had a baby, Gayle's grandfather. So Gayle and I were first cousins once removed, if that was the right term.

"I'm wondering if you're okay." She turned sideways in her desk to get a better look at me and stretched her long, dark legs into the aisle.

I shrugged and gathered my books. "Yeah, I'm just nervous about my date with David, Saturday." That was part of the truth.

Her full lips formed a wide grin between her brown cheeks. "Why? It'll be great." She reached over and tapped my arm.

That coaxed a smile out of me. "It probably will. Are you going to the parade?"

"Maybe. I'm trying to find out if Bear will be there."

The bell rang, and we parted for our last classes of the day.

Gayle's secret crush on the giant football player called Bear was sweet. If he didn't notice her soon, her heart might break. I couldn't stand the thought of heartbreak for anyone I loved.

Friday morning before school, Alice and I found Mom drinking coffee in the kitchen.

"Happy Birthday, Mom."

"Happy Birthday, Mama C."

"Thanks, sweeties." She set her cup down and wrapped an arm around each of us.

Papa D had planned to take us out to eat that evening but apologized to Alice and me that we'd be celebrating at home instead. He and Mom had probably decided together, Mom being as thrifty and frugal as she was. Even more now, with the layoff situation.

"Guess what?" Her eyes sparkled. "I have an interview this afternoon."

"Really?" So fast! I clapped my hands.

"Yep. I saw an ad in the newspaper Monday and called about it."

"Great, Mama C."

I had to give Alice credit for not letting her disappointment over music camp affect the way she treated our parents.

"We'll have some fun this evening after your interview." I wanted her to know we planned to do something for her birthday.

"Of course we will. I can't wait." She smiled as she stood and carried her cup to the sink. "Don't be late for the bus."

She headed toward the garage.

I scooted to the pantry. Facing Alice, I held up a white cake mix in one hand and a yellow one in the other. "This is all we have to choose from."

Alice opened and closed kitchen cabinet doors until she spied the electric mixer. "I can't believe we forgot about a cake. We'll have to get started right after school if it's gonna be ready by the time she comes back from her interview."

"And we don't have any frosting." I grimaced, exposing my clamped-together teeth.

"I can make some."

"You can?" My eyebrows lifted.

"Of course. I've been making chocolate frosting for years. We have cocoa, powdered sugar, and butter, don't we?"

I nodded.

"Problem solved."

At times like these I was grateful Alice had been the woman of her house after her mother died.

"Sh-sh." I waved at Alice to stop talking as Mom passed the kitchen carrying a painted nightstand from the garage.

I craned my neck to make sure she kept going. "I'll

mix up the batter as soon as we get home."

"Good. I'll call my dad so he doesn't buy a cake at the grocery store. I love him, but he never picks a good one."

Alice and I made chicken salad from canned chicken for dinner, and Adam set the table. The cake sat on top of the refrigerator, and all the gifts waited in my room.

By the time Mom hit the door after her interview, Papa D pulled into the drive.

Alice, Adam, and I met Mom as she kicked off her high heels and dropped her bag and suit jacket into a living room chair.

Adam squeezed her around her middle. "I love you, Mama C. I'm so glad you're home."

"I love you too, Adam." She grinned over his head at Alice and me.

"You look so pretty, Mom. Happy Birthday—again." I hugged her.

Alice hugged her, too. "How did the interview go?"

Mom's eyes brightened as she loosened the collar on her blouse. "Pretty well, actually. They'll let me know next week."

"That's great," Alice and I chirped.

Mom took a deep breath. "Do I smell cake? The aroma is heavenly, and I'm starved." She pattered on stocking feet toward the kitchen with Adam trailing behind her.

"You have to eat your dinner first!" I yelled after them.

"The chicken salad was delicious, girls. Thank you so much." Mom got up and went around the table to give each of us a kiss on the cheek.

"You're welcome, Mom." I distributed the dessert plates.

"I helped set the table," Adam yelled, wiggling in his chair.

"You did a great job, too." Mom kissed him the hardest, accompanied by a big "Mwa!"

"Now it's party time!" Alice left for the kitchen and returned with the cake.

Papa D brought in the gifts and cards.

We stood to sing "Happy Birthday," and Mom blew out the candles, of which there were three. Nobody remembered to buy extras, but maybe she would rather not have seen thirty-nine candles anyway.

"Why don't you open the kids' gifts first?" Papa D held Adam back so Mom could choose without interference. "It's *her* birthday," he whispered to Adam.

She chose the big gift bag from Alice and me. I handed her the card, and she read it.

"Ohhh, how sweet. Thank you, girls." She looked up, eyes misty.

Alice's face turned pink. "You're welcome, Mama C."

I loved the way Alice treated Mom. I hoped she felt like a real daughter.

"Come on, Mom, look in the bag." I bounced, more than ready for her to see her gift.

She extracted the jewelry box and gasped, her eyes widening. "This is the most beautiful jewelry box I have ever seen." And she broke down bawling.

The last thing I wanted to do was make her cry. "Mom, what's wrong?"

Papa D stood up. "Honey?"

"It's just so unexpected." She sniffed and wiped her tears with a paper napkin.

I rubbed her shoulder. "I'll go get some of Grand-mère Robichaud's jewelry you've been keeping in those cardboard boxes. It'll fit so nicely in here."

She grabbed my arm. "Wait."

My mouth opened. The look in her eyes—what was the problem?

"I'm sorry to tell you this, Wendy, but I sold most of it."

I gasped. "Sold?" My legs wobbled, and I grabbed a chair. "Mom."

"Please don't be angry." It was almost a whisper.

"Why did you do that?" I glanced at Papa D, who looked as surprised as I was. Alice and Adam sat as still as statues, their eyes huge.

"I wanted to pay off some debt to make our budget easier to manage." She bit her lip.

"Which pieces?" My heart felt stuck like a pincushion. "Not her pendant watch, I hope." My trembling hand covered my crucifix as though it might leap from my neck to the pawnshop or wherever she took the other jewelry.

"Unfortunately, that was one of them." Her voice deepened. "Your grand-mère gave it to me, and I thought she wouldn't mind if I sold it under the circumstances."

"I was hoping to inherit that." I squeezed my eyes shut and rattled my head. Dad would be so mad at her if he found out about this.

"But I kept the pearls." The tone of her voice lifted, hopeful. "I thought those would be more useful to you as you got older."

I huffed and blinked back tears. No wonder the jewelry box was such a shock to her.

"I love my gift, sweetie. It was wonderfully thoughtful." She placed a hand over mine. "We'll have other family treasures to place in it in the future."

I nodded. But everything was spinning out of control. I didn't trust the future anymore. And I should've saved my money toward a trip to Alaska instead of wasting it on a big jewelry box nobody needed.

Mom opened the rest of her gifts, and Alice focused on the cake as she sliced and dished it up.

It tasted like cardboard in my mouth as conversation hummed around me.

"You ladies are probably tired," Papa D said. "I'll clear the table."

I shoved my chair back and ran to my room.

Chapter 3

The next morning, I slept late, the best way to postpone thinking about the loss of Grand-mère Robichaud's treasures—my treasures.

Warm water blasted my face in the shower. I should've asked in advance for the pendant watch for my fifteenth birthday like I'd planned. Now I'd be lucky if I got anything as a gift.

I'm sorry, God. Not only was I being selfish, but it wasn't true—or fair. Even when we had practically nothing, Mom always had a gift for me on special occasions.

I dressed in jeans topped with a pink and purple printed

t-shirt and a green scarf to complete the Mardi Gras colors. I arrived in the kitchen as Mom and Papa D finished breading and frying shrimp for po-boys. They put on a good act of behaving normally, smiling and pecking each other on the cheek. But when the cooking ended, Mom stared at the platter of shrimp with a faraway look in her eyes.

The shrimp smelled good, but no way could I eat. My nerves made me as jumpy as a flea found on Belle when she was a puppy last summer. Papa D's job loss, Alice's gloominess over band camp, Mom's selling the jewelry— enough to ruin anyone's appetite. Topping those with spending an afternoon with David's whole family for the first time didn't help.

Everyone else worked at the counter to build a po-boy on French bread, dressing it with lettuce, tomato, and mayonnaise. Well, all Adam added was the mayo.

I perched on a stool and stared at the lettuce leaf, tomato slice, and two shrimp on my plate. David had said his mom would have stuff for us to eat before the parade anyway in case I got hungry later.

The dogs trolled at our feet. Belle and her mother Chanceaux, Mrs. V's dog we took in when Mrs. V moved, watched for something edible to fall to the floor.

With ten minutes remaining before David and his family would pick me up, I tossed the tomato slice into my mouth. I gave each of the dogs one of my shrimp and left to brush my teeth. In the bathroom, I checked my hair and makeup and misted myself with fragrance.

The front doorbell rang. Chanceaux and Belle barked until I answered the door and they recognized David.

"Hi, David. Come in." I loved his face all scrubbed and shiny. A whiff of herbal shampoo, and I fought the urge to run my fingers through his curly brown hair.

He grinned and blushed. "Hey. You look great."

"Thanks. So do you." I reached around him and closed the door.

He leaned in really close. "It kills me the way your brown eyes have those little flecks of green that show up sometimes. Like on a sunny day or when you wear certain colors."

Sparks fired from my skin.

Chanceaux's and Belle's tails beat against our legs as they waited for attention. David bent down and patted their yellow and honey-colored coats. Satisfied, the dogs scampered off to the kitchen to beg for scraps again.

David straightened and slapped hair from his palms. "Are you ready?"

"I am, but would you say hello to my parents? They're in the kitchen."

"Sure." He stepped a few feet in and waved toward the archway to the kitchen. "Hi, Mr. and Mrs. Rend."

Mom and Papa D spoke in unison. "Hello, David."

Papa D set down his glass. "What time will you have Wendy back?"

"It'll be late this afternoon. We'll probably stop for ice cream after the parade. Is that okay?"

"That's fine," Mom said. "Please thank your parents for letting Wendy join you."

"I will."

I wiggled my fingers in good-bye. David and I slipped out the door.

He took my hand for the walk to his family's SUV. "Is your stepfather going to the parade? He's an Air Force veteran, isn't he? Maybe they have a float."

I hadn't given it a thought, but I didn't know Papa D last year at this time. "That's right. He is a veteran, but …

"But what?"

"I guess he doesn't feel like going."

Or maybe he was afraid of running into people who knew he'd lost his job.

Unlike the wild celebrations in New Orleans, our Mardi Gras parade drew families with kids. And everyone kept their clothes on, except an occasional toddler who lost a diaper. The parade always finished at the park so the fun could continue. David's dad had set us up near the end of the route so we only had a short walk to meet up with David's grandfather at the park.

The crowd swelled as other parade-watchers reached us. The blue-note writer could've been anyone among them. He could've been walking right behind me!

I spun around, startling a lady in a floppy hat. A man wearing reflective sunglasses stared at me. Well, as much as I could tell.

No good reason existed not to search for pairs of people who looked like they planned a meeting instead of accidentally running into each other. The park wasn't very big. I might be able to spot the two people connected by the jewelry-box note if the note referred to this year's parade. But I didn't know whether the individuals were male or female, friends or enemies. I had no clue about the type of rendezvous it hinted at. Which made me wonder if the meeting fit the category of legal.

Whenever one person walked up to another one more than a few yards away, I raised a hand to my brow and squinted into the distance.

"Is something wrong?" David frowned.

My hand had moved up his arm, my fingernails digging into his skin.

"No. Sorry." I relaxed my grip, slid my hand back into his, and took a deep breath.

A date with David and his family was hardly the time or place to run around like a goose looking for someone or something that might not exist. Or—and I hated to admit it—something that might not be any of my business. *Might not? It wasn't.* That had never stopped me before, but still, my dates with David were too precious to waste the time I could spend with him.

David and I accompanied his parents to a shady area of the park to wait for his grandfather to find us. David's brother, Ben, and Ben's girlfriend, Carla, split from us and wandered off. They blended into the crowd as a band in the gazebo played its first tune.

A lot of improvements had been made to the park since I'd enjoyed its heavy-duty swings as a kid. A new picnic area with tables quickly filled with families.

People moved along the new landscaped walking

paths. Faces I hadn't seen since eighth grade popped into view every few seconds to be lost again in the throng before I could make my way toward them.

"Hey, Wendy!" Jennifer yelled and waved her whole arm until I thought the shoulder joint would separate and her arm would fall off. In a crowd of people mostly our age, she stood out, moving in that ballerina way of walking she had, with long strides and toes pointed outward. A breezy dress in her best color, sky blue, swished around her knees as her golden blonde hair fluttered against her shoulders. She clutched the arm of a cute guy a little older looking than ninth grade, one I didn't recognize. Maybe he attended another high school.

"Hi, Jen." I waved back. Once best friends, Jennifer and I had grown apart since eighth grade, but I missed her cheerful personality and the way it helped me forget my troubles. A familiar urge to confide in her swept through me.

She and the guy passed, so they no longer faced me. Jennifer half-turned around and grinned open-mouthed, pointing at him from behind and bobbing her head up and down.

I laughed and nodded. I should call her and see if we could get together soon. We shared one class the current semester and occasionally ran into each other in the cafeteria, but we could use a private chat.

David squinted at the backs of their heads and scowled.

Alarm prickled my skin. "Do you know him?"

He shook his head. "Nah. I think I've seen him somewhere before, but I'm not sure where."

Together we watched the pair as they disappeared in the crowd.

"Let's take a walk and search for my grandpa." He led me down a path that curved under large oak trees shading a row of iron benches.

I touched his arm. "David, look, there's Mr. Stanley."

Our eighth-grade English teacher sat alone, his arms stretched across the back of a bench, one ankle crossed over a knee. As relaxed as I'd ever seen his bulldog face, he stared straight ahead.

"He was one of my favorite teachers. Let's go say hello."

David groaned.

"Come on." I grabbed his hand and yanked.

We approached from the side. "Hello, Mr. Stanley." I used a sophisticated tone and gave him my most mature smile.

He blinked and turned his head toward me but didn't change position on the bench.

"Well, hello, Wendy. David." He spoke slowly, his eyebrows twitching like we'd interrupted his private thoughts. "How are you?"

I hesitated a split second. "Fine." Why did every conversation since learning about Papa D's problem make me feel like I was keeping a dark secret—or lying?

Mr. Stanley's gaze wandered toward the people milling about.

"You know, you're still the best English teacher I've ever had." I'd never told him how much I enjoyed his class.

"That's nice of you to say." He pushed his glasses up the bridge of his nose. "It's good seeing you. Take care."

My face warmed. That was as much of a dismissal as if the bell had rung.

David tugged my arm. "We need to get going. Nice seeing you, Mr. Stanley."

We traveled out of earshot, and I whispered, "Did you hear him? How rude."

"I think we just caught him at a bad time. Maybe he needed some privacy."

I sighed. Guys understood one another like I probably never would. "Yeah, I guess." But I'd always held teachers to a higher standard, expecting them to behave better than everyone else.

David squeezed my hand and made a naval-warning whistle through his teeth. "Grandfather straight ahead."

An older man talked with David's parents near the gazebo. We slowed our pace on the approach, focused on the group.

A hard tap on my shoulder from behind startled me, and I stopped. Frowning, I turned around. So did David.

"Melissa?" Of course I recognized her. Nearly-black, silky-straight hair. Almond-shaped eyes as dark as her hair. Why would the perfect-looking leader of the fashionable Sticks want to be seen with me? Especially at a public event.

Her glossy pink lips didn't smile. "Can I talk to you for a second?" It wasn't a request but more of a command. "Alone."

I switched to high-alert mode. It wasn't that I'd had any run-ins with her. And she could be pleasant when she chose to be. But I'd seen her reduce a girl to tears with a single comment about her clothes or weight.

"I'll catch up with you in a minute, David. Please ask your grandfather not to leave. I really want to meet him." I kissed his cheek.

David glanced warily at Melissa. "Sure." He stuffed his hands into his pockets and stalked off.

"What do you want?" I placed one hand on my hip.

"You're still good at English, right?"

"Yeah."

"The writing part?"

I narrowed my eyes to slits and nodded slowly, dropping my hand to my side.

"I need a tutor."

My eyes popped open and eyebrows shot upward. "For pay?"

"Yeah, but I don't want anyone at LeMoyne to know I hired one."

Ah, the perfect Melissa had a weak spot to hide. "They don't have to."

"So you'll do it? You'll tutor me?"

I chewed my lip for a sec. She wasn't someone I'd ordinarily choose to have any kind of relationship with— business or otherwise. But she appeared desperate. And she was known to have money, which I needed.

"On two conditions." I crossed my arms. "We'll have to agree in advance on a fee, and you'll have to come to my house for the sessions. I have other obligations."

"Agreed."

"I'll think it over tonight and cover the details with you at school tomorrow."

"But just don't—"

"I know. Find you when the other Sti—when your friends aren't around."

"Okay." She departed as quickly as she'd appeared.

This could be the answer to my prayers. With a light step, I joined the Griffin family. Ben and Carla had reconnected with the group.

"Grandpa, this is Wendy." A big grin covered David's face as he reached out and pulled me to his side.

Sweet. He was proud of me.

"Great to meet you, Wendy. I've heard nice things about you." His eyes were the same green as David's, his hair the same curly brown, but with gray at the sides and streaked throughout. I'd seen him before, maybe at school?

"You too, Mr. Griffin."

He offered his right hand. "Call me George."

I took it. "Okay, George."

He placed his other hand over mine. "I heard you're an artist, and you run track. Is that right?"

"Yes."

"So you and David are both athletes. Will you go to any of his baseball games?"

"I plan to try."

"Great. I'll see you there. And I hope David brings you around more often."

"Thank you." I glanced at David, who blushed.

George clapped him on the shoulder. "You remember where I live?"

David rolled his eyes. "Of course, Grandpa."

George tapped palms against his chest. "Well, folks, thanks to all of you for coming out and cheering for my float. I enjoyed the company, but I don't want to keep you." He shook hands with David's dad and with Ben. He kissed David's mom on the cheek.

"Don't you want to go with us for ice cream?" she asked.

"No, I'm going to hang around here a little while and take in the sights."

"He means the ladies," David whispered to me.

I chuckled. "It was nice meeting you, George."

"Same here, Wendy." He turned to David and opened his arms. David hugged him.

"'Bye, Grandpa." David watched him for a few seconds as the older man waved and walked away.

David's dad placed an arm around his wife. "Okay, who's ready for ice cream?"

The rest of us spoke in unison, "I am," and then we laughed. We followed David's parents to the SUV and climbed in.

I sat close to David but resisted the urge to snuggle in front of his parents. "Your grandfather's nice. Have I seen him before?"

"Probably." He paused and squeezed his eyebrows together. "At school last year, maybe. He attended a parent-teacher conference and some other events when my dad was working out of state."

"Oh, I think I remember seeing him talk to Mrs. Perez in homeroom."

"That sounds right."

Satisfied with clearing my question up, I placed my hand in his. My thoughts wandered to Melissa's hidden weakness and how I might capitalize on it.

David and I sauntered toward my front door, arms touching and fingers woven together. Enough daylight remained for us to be seen, so what kind of kiss—if any— would he give me with his parents watching? Would it be as sweet as the last one? Or the first one?

He must've read my mind. He glanced toward the SUV, smirked, and blushed. But just the same, he leaned in and brushed my lips with his.

Value based on quality contact per second: Excellent.

And I admired bravery.

That had to be the best family group date ever. David had been such a good boyfriend to invite me to the parade.

A wave rose in my chest. Did that make us officially a couple again? If I was the first girl he'd ever included in a family activity …

My heart sprouted wings, believing I was the first. Which had to make me officially his girlfriend.

I sighed. I should ask him to do something with my family next, but not too soon. Not right after the date for the parade. And it was too soon after Papa D lost his job. The atmosphere wasn't exactly upbeat around the house and neither were its inhabitants. But something was bound to come up that I could invite him to. I'd keep my ears open.

The blue note lay on my dresser, folded over once to casually conceal its message. It shuddered in the breeze from my ceiling fan.

That blue paper.

My chest vibrated as if a wave crashed against its wall.

I inhaled a long breath. The paper was the color of Jennifer's dress at the park— her favorite color. Sky blue. The same color as the stationery she'd used to write to me last summer during her dance workshop in New York. Had someone written a note to Jennifer using her favorite color? Or did she write the note to give to someone and then forget about it?

My stomach tilted like a wrecked wooden pirogue in a bayou.

That guy Jennifer was with—did they exchange a note so she'd meet him on the sly? He looked older than us. How long had she been seeing him? Where was he from? What kind of person was he?

My feelings for Jennifer rushed back. She was still my friend deep down inside, and I cared what happened to her.

But the jewelry box. I'd never seen one like it in her room. Of course, I hadn't visited her room since the end of last summer.

Maybe I should call and ask—ask her what? If she's sneaking around behind her parents' backs? If she's serious about that guy? If he's trouble?

Maybe I could find out more at school if I hung around her ballerina friends and listened. Maybe David would remember where he'd seen the guy.

My alarm clock read eight o'clock. The evening was slipping by. If I spent it worrying about Jennifer and her new boyfriend, I wouldn't be any closer to solving the mystery than if I hadn't.

And I still needed to formulate a plan for tutoring Melissa in English. I had to figure out how much time we'd need, when to meet, and what to charge her. If she needed help with "the writing part," she probably didn't know where to begin. Developing a topic could take a lot of time. Not everyone was creative.

The English teachers usually gave writing assignments from a few days to a few weeks in advance of their due date. The next one for our class was due the week before school let out for spring break. If Melissa and I met twice a week for an hour, we should be able to cover that assignment and anything else that came up and get it turned in on time. If we didn't have an assignment due, I could use the sessions to coach her so she'd learn to think and create on her own. Once a week might turn out to be enough, but if I priced my services per week, no matter how many times we met, I'd be guaranteed regular income.

I rubbed my eyes and located a notepad and pencil. Estimating what Melissa might be willing to pay per week, I figured out how much I could make by the end of the school year.

If I saved and added all my allowance to those earnings, I might be able to pay for half of one plane ticket to Anchorage by summer. I'd worry about getting the other half another way.

And Alice's music camp? She was on her own.

Chapter 4

"We need to run together this week to condition for track." Gayle widened her eyes until the cocoa-bean brown was surrounded by white, while she bobbed her head up and down.

A laugh burst from my mouth, sending a wave of air right at her. "Are you a carnival mystic trying to control my mind, or is something wrong with your new contact lenses?"

She waved both hands in front of her face like I had bad breath. Which I didn't, because I'd used mouthwash after breakfast.

I pulled some books for Monday morning classes out of my locker. "I know we need to train early for track season, but isn't that what practice is for?"

"Don't you know how hard the coaches will work us?" Her voice rose to its highest pitch. "I don't want to be sore."

"Well, then, let's agree to get together one afternoon this week."

"Two." She turned her head of bouncy black curls and shouted, "Alice! Don't you want to run?"

"Right now?" Alice trudged toward her locker. "I can barely walk with this load. Good thing I leave my clarinet in the music room every morning." She swung a book bag from her shoulder, and it thudded to the floor.

Gayle sighed. "I'm talking about the three of us running this week."

"Sure. I need to start before I get fat. Again."

I rolled my eyes. "You were never fat. You have a muscular build. Besides, you shed twenty pounds like that …" I snapped my fingers. "… when you started running."

"Well, I say we do it." Alice swapped books between her bag and locker. "The sooner, the better."

A grin stretched across Gayle's face. "Great. Why don't we meet at the park? It's about equal distance between my house and yours."

"That sounds good, don't you think, Wendy?" Alice lowered her voice and cocked a blonde eyebrow. "And it's something that's free."

I gave her a sharp glance. She'd better not blab about our financial situation to anyone, not even Gayle.

"So, which day do we start?" Gayle pressed her lips together in a determined line.

My potential deal with Melissa didn't allow a commitment just yet. "I'll have to let you know a little later when I'm sure which days I have available." I picked up my books and left them staring at me.

If it were possible for anyone to make earth science more attractive, that person would be David.

"In the northern hemisphere, hurricanes spin counterclockwise. In the southern hemisphere, clockwise." He demonstrated with twirls of an index finger, to the snorts and guffaws of the other guys.

From the looks on some of the girls' faces, they thought he was as adorable as I did.

That's how it was every day. David's enthusiasm for rocks, atmosphere, and ocean currents turned up his cute factor at the same time it shamed me into participating when the teacher asked a question. Who could act bored with somebody like that sitting next to her? He and I would make such a cute scientific couple wearing matching khaki shorts with white t-shirts and working together collecting rock samples or flying into a tropical storm …

The bell rang. David rose from his desk and stretched muscular arms over his head. "So what about Saturday?"

"Hmm?" I reached into my purse for some breath mints and offered him one.

"Ben and Carla invited us to go on a picnic with them."

"Oh, sure. That sounds like fun." I popped a mint into my mouth and gathered my books. "It's nice of them to ask us to double again."

"Ben feels sorry for me because I can't drive and take you anywhere. Besides, he says they had a good time with us at the movies last time. Carla really likes you, by the way, and she's particular."

I grinned and squeezed a shoulder toward my cheek as we walked out the door. "So we have something in common."

We stopped in the hall before splitting ways.

I turned to David. "Where will we go?"

"The park."

Everybody wanted me to go to the park. It was as though God was making sure I'd be back.

At lunch I slowly passed the ballerina table with my ears perked, trying not to catch anyone's eye. The girls' high-pitched chatter swelled like the sounds from a nest of hatchlings waiting for a worm. It was impossible to pick up on anything about Jennifer's boyfriend amidst all the noise.

I'd probably have to ask her if I wanted to find out. Maybe phoning would be best.

Alice gave me a nod toward an empty table. Gayle and I reached it at the same time and flanked Alice at one end.

Seated with the other Sticks across the cafeteria, Melissa kept an eye on me the whole time I ate. If she put any food in her mouth, I didn't notice. No wonder she stayed so skinny.

When I finished, I hurried to the restroom with fifteen minutes to spare before my next class. I'd catch up with Melissa and get our arrangement settled in time.

I came out of the stall and almost slammed into her. Without making a sound, she appeared right in front of me, like a vampire in a movie—with her black hair and dressed all in black.

I gasped. "Melissa."

She stooped and checked under the stalls. "What kind of deal are you offering?" She straightened back up.

The vampire was all business.

I had a figure ready on a slip of paper in my pocket. I handed it to her. "This much per week, paid cash in advance."

She pursed her lips and glared at me.

"It's the same price each week whether we meet once, twice, or three times. You can decide how much help you need."

Her features relaxed.

"I can't predict our assignments, but I figure we can try meeting on Tuesdays and Fridays at first. That would cover us if we get an assignment on Friday that's due Monday, or if we get an assignment Monday or Tuesday that's due toward the end of the week. We can switch from Friday to Thursday when we need to."

"Okay then." She stuffed the note into her jeans. "My sister can drop me off after school, and my mom can pick me up on her way home from work."

"All right. We can start tomorrow."

We exchanged phone numbers, and she jotted down

my address.

I was all set for the trip to Alaska becoming a reality, except I hadn't asked Mom or Papa D for permission to turn our house into a learning center. With any luck, they'd be too busy looking for work to worry about it.

World history—not English class— produced the first writing project for Melissa and me to tackle. Essays on our favorite ancient civilizations were due Friday.

"I'll catch up with you," Melissa told her Stick friends when class dismissed. They obediently filed into the hall.

"Think about the ancient civilizations, and pick one before we meet." In an authoritative manner, I lifted my chin and looked down my nose at her. Quite a feat because my height exceeded hers by an inch, if that much.

Didn't work. She shrugged and left the room.

All afternoon, I listened everywhere I went for any information about Jennifer and *that guy*, as I referred to him in my thoughts.

Nothing. For being so talkative, Jennifer and the ballerinas sure were tight-lipped about him.

"David, do you remember when we saw Jennifer with

that guy at the park?" We walked the hall between classes.

"Yeah, why?" He got a look on his face guys get when they sense you're going to talk about chick stuff.

"Where have you met him before? Can you remember?"

He blew air out of his lungs. "No. Well … yeah."

"What?"

He cut his eyes at me.

This was ridiculous. Was I going to have to pull it out of him?

"I didn't actually meet him. Ben had gone to a party. This was before he had his own car, and I was with Dad when we picked him up. That guy was standing outside in the front yard."

"And?"

"Ben was ticked off. He'd called Dad to pick him up early because some of the guys had alcohol and were getting drunk. That guy was one of them."

"Oh, no." I grabbed David by the arm and made him stop. "I've got to talk to Jennifer."

He raised an open palm. "Okay, wait. Think before you run off and say something you'll regret."

I gritted my teeth. He was right. If I opened my big Bird Face mouth and stuck my foot in it … "Do you think she was at the party?"

He shook his head. "I doubt it. That was last school year. Her parents wouldn't have let her go to a party with high school kids, would they?"

"No. But if she doesn't know he drinks, she needs to know. And if she knows—" My stomach flipped like a crab cake on a spatula.

"Just wait and don't do anything yet. Maybe I can find out more. I'll see you later, okay?" He pecked me on the cheek while no teacher was looking and headed toward his class.

I remained glued to the spot, my mind whirling. If only Jen and I had stayed close since the summer. Did she wish it, too?

The second bell rang, and I dashed ahead.

Tomorrow Melissa was coming over after school. But sometime this week I had to get over to Jennifer's to talk to her.

Without fail.

On the bus ride home, I explained to Alice the arrangement I had with Melissa and told her not to tell anyone.

She ducked her chin and pointed a cool blue gaze up at me. "Seriously? Melissa. Of Sticks fame."

"You know, instead of being critical, maybe you should try to make some money, too." I cocked my head and raised one eyebrow.

"And what would happen if both our parents wound up getting a job? I have a little brother to take care of." She turned toward the window and muttered under her breath, "And so do you."

I sighed. Shirking responsibility I'd agreed to wasn't me. But this cash cow—Melissa would have a fit if she heard that—was too good to give up. A limited number of hours in the day were available after school and on weekends. I simply had to make this work. What other options were there to bring in money fast enough by summer?

Just because Alice couldn't have an after-school job didn't mean I shouldn't. Why shouldn't I take advantage of this opportunity to get to Alaska that happened to drop into my lap?

But if Alice expected me to share my money with her for music camp, she was crazy. She'd better save her allowance like I was saving mine. And why couldn't she sell something? If I had to lose some of Grand-mère's jewelry to help keep the family afloat, Alice could do without some of her belongings, too.

My chest gave a flutter like a hummingbird was trapped inside.

I'd save my allowance—if Mom and Papa D didn't decide it was the next thing to go.

After dinner, I phoned Jennifer. It wasn't until she answered that I was struck by just how much I had missed hearing her voice every day. Especially with Alice and me not getting along.

"Wendy! I was just thinking about you." She sparkled with her trademark cheer.

"Oh, yeah? How?"

"I'll have two extra tickets to my spring dance recital. Do you think you'd want them?"

My heart warmed. She hadn't forgotten me completely. "Yes, I would."

"Great! It'll be fun to see you there. Just like old times. I'll give them to you when they come in."

"Thanks, Jen."

6 Dates to Disaster

"Maybe you could ask Daa-vid." She giggled.

"Maybe." My voice sounded high and noncommittal.

"Oh, I'm sorry. I've been hogging the conversation. I didn't mean to take total control. Why did you call? You must've called about something."

I waited a moment until I was sure she'd finished. "Actually, I was wondering if I could come over one afternoon this week."

Seconds of silence passed. "Um, suuure."

What a lukewarm response. And after her excited reaction to my call. "If you have other plans, that's okay." *Please don't, please don't, please don't.* I clenched my teeth.

"No, not the whole week."

The gears turning in her head were all but audible. That guy had to be the reason.

She cleared her throat. "Which day?"

"How about Wednesday?" I crossed my fingers.

"I think that'll be fine." Weak, but still agreement.

"Good. I'll see you as soon as I can bike over after I get off the bus."

"Okay." She paused. "Wendy?"

"Yeah?"

"I'm glad you called," she said softly.

"Me too."

She definitely had something on her mind. With any luck, I'd get her to spill it.

Chapter 5

Alice and I had barely gotten off the bus Tuesday when Melissa's older sister dropped her at the house. I led her to my room and asked her to wait while I hunted for Mom.

Paintbrush in hand, Mom squatted in the garage next to a headboard lying on newspapers. One of the neighbors had put it out with the trash.

Chanceaux and Belle lay nearby. They beat their tails against the cement floor as I entered the garage.

The back of Mom's head looked so sweet while she worked. I couldn't stay mad at her about Grand-mère's jewelry. How could I, when she'd always tried so hard to be thrifty to the point of doing without new things for my sake? She wouldn't have sold any of that jewelry if she hadn't needed to.

"Mom?"

"Hi, sweetie." She didn't turn around. "Home from school already? I didn't realize it was so late."

"My friend Melissa is here." *Friend.* I controlled a snort. "We're working on an assignment together."

"That's good, honey. I'm trying to get all the bedroom furniture finished in case I get a callback about a job soon." She dipped her brush and tapped it on the edge of the paint can.

"Where's Papa D?"

"Out looking. Say a prayer for us both, okay?"

"Okay, I will. I'm gonna grab a snack for Melissa and me."

Confident I'd get no interference or interruption from either of my parents, I headed to the kitchen. Adam had arrived home, and Alice started fixing him a snack. I picked up two water bottles and a bag of potato chips and hurried back to my room.

"Which civilization did you choose to write about?" I extended a bottle toward Melissa, who took it.

"The Qin Dynasty in China."

I groaned inwardly. Why couldn't she pick one I know something about? "I don't remember that one."

"Maybe you don't have any Chinese ancestors." She batted her eyelids.

"Right." We were off to a roaring good start.

"It doesn't matter anyway, because I have a list of facts I got off the Internet. I just need you to help me write the thing."

Uh-huh.

I sat at my computer, and she at the wooden dining chair with peeling paint I'd taken from the garage. She pulled closer to me. I typed her list of facts into a Word document, and we began to compose them into a paper. Well, she tried to begin. And tried. And tried.

Finally, I began. Because, wow, did Melissa ever need help. As Grand-mère Robichaud used to say, "Mais, talk about!"

I'd hoped to get her started and then work on my own composition about ancient Rome. But ninety minutes passed just coaching her on how to take those facts about the Qin dynasty, put them together into sentences, and arrange those sentences in some kind of order that made sense. And that didn't leave time to make the composition any less than boring.

"We're not there yet." I shook my head and saved the document on my computer.

Melissa pouted her glossy pink lips.

"I'll email this version to you. You can look it over tomorrow and maybe think of some ways to spice it up. Then save your version with a 'two' at the end and send it back to me."

"That's what I'm paying you for—to spice it up. I'll be back on Thursday so we can finish."

I was too tired to argue.

We called it an evening, stretched, and took a bathroom break. Melissa's mom showed up fifteen minutes later to get her. I emailed the document to her, just in case she got inspired.

All my homework awaited me, but I trekked to the backyard to visit with the dogs while Mom cooked dinner. I needed a diversion.

Working for Melissa was harder than I expected. And a lot harder than babysitting, where I could tackle my assignments while the kids watched TV.

The money was definitely better, but …

What had I gotten myself into?

Chapter 6

All day Wednesday, Jennifer and I exchanged grins in passing. She had to be as excited as I was about getting together.

I shrugged off a twinge of guilt about my real reason for calling her. Who should care? We were going to hang out together again. I worried about her, so my deception made it okay, didn't it?

After school, Mom wasn't home, wouldn't you know it.

"Alice, I'll feed the dogs if you can fix Adam's snack." I stuffed a folded slice of cheddar into my mouth and reached for the bag of dog chow in the pantry.

"Why are you in such a hurry?" She placed cheese on

slices of bread.

I gulped down the cheese. "I sort of have an appointment at Jennifer's."

"You're kidding, right?"

I straightened, dog chow in hand.

She slid the bread into the toaster oven. "I thought we planned on running with Gayle today."

Shoot! I squeezed my eyes tight and grimaced. "Did we decide on today?"

"Yeah. And Mama C is coming home to watch Adam."

"I'm sorry. It slipped my mind."

Alice sighed. "I'll see if Gayle can change it to tomorrow."

A groan bellowed from my throat, and my head dropped backward, then forward again. "Melissa's coming back tomorrow."

Alice opened her mouth as if to speak. The toaster oven dinged, and she turned toward it.

I dropped the bag and reached for her shoulder. "Go without me today. Please. I promise I'll join you Friday."

She turned around and gave me a small nod, her blue irises cloudy. "Adam, snack's ready!"

The dogs followed me to the laundry room where I

poured food into their dishes. I put away the bag, filled their water bowl, and hurried out to the garage for my bike.

Riding into my old neighborhood to see Jen brought back so many memories of Jen and me—and of Mrs. V, too. The fun things I used to do with them. Jen and I finding and caring for Chanceaux and her litter of puppies. Mrs. V's cookies and her scrambled egg sandwiches. I didn't know it at the time, but those were some of the best years of my life.

My nose burned from tears threatening to surface.

Stop it, Wendy. You're being a big baby. Things change. People change and move on.

Yep. And at least I'd be with Jen this afternoon.

My spirits lifted like they always used to when I turned onto her street.

Nearing the house, I slowed and did a double-take. Was that the same house? Jen's yard and front porch— always the prettiest on the street—were full of junk. And the grass needed mowing.

I coasted up the driveway, past an old wooden rocking chair, a chest of drawers, and a bench. What was going on?

I dismounted and parked my bike.

Weaving my way on foot around smaller items on the porch, I looked them over. None of this stuff reflected the clean, modern look of the interior of Jen's house I remembered.

The front door swung open just as I raised my hand to ring the bell.

"Hey." Jen's hair fluttered from the sudden movement of air. "Pardon the mess."

"No problem." I stepped over the threshold. "Where'd all the stuff come from?"

"The attic and closets, mostly."

Including an old jewelry box, perhaps? I peered more closely at the items surrounding my feet.

"And my Sampson grandparents moved from their big old house into a condo. Mom and Dad brought back everything that wouldn't fit."

"What are you going to do with it all?" Not that my mother needed any more refurbishing projects. Plus, our house had filled quickly with two families' worth of stuff.

"A Salvation Army truck is coming today to pick up the big pieces outside. I think we're going to have a yard sale this Saturday for the smaller stuff."

"Sounds like a good idea." I hugged her. "Well, how

have you been? Other than what I can guess at school?" I cringed inside. Not very subtle, but how could she know my mind?

"I'll tell you." She took my hand like when we were kids and led me toward her room. "There's more to why we're getting rid of stuff in the attic. I'm glad you called because there's something I've wanted you to know, but I wasn't sure if you'd even care after all this time."

"Of course I'd care." My words rattled in my throat as she towed me along.

In her room, she spun around to face me and took a deep breath, her blue eyes big and hopeful. "We're moving when school lets out for summer."

"You mean … to a new house or …?"

She scrunched her mouth and nose. "To the city. My dad got a promotion and …" She shrugged.

My legs wobbled as if one of those gnomes standing on her front porch had punched me in the knees. "So this is our last school year together."

"Yeah." Her voice was soft.

"I'm happy for you, I guess." I forced a little smile. "But I'll miss you. A lot of people will."

"I'll miss you, too, even though we haven't spent much time together since last summer."

"We'll just have to make up for that before you leave."

"Yes, we will." She hugged me tight and then pulled back, hanging onto my wrists. "There is one good thing about moving I wanted to tell you."

"What's that?"

Pink flooded her cheeks and her eyes sparkled. "I'll go to the same school as my new boyfriend. You saw him with me the day of the Mardi Gras parade."

My jaw dropped the same time my stomach did. *No!*

Her blonde eyebrows pushed together above her nose, and she released my wrists.

My eyes darted from side to side as I searched for the right thing to say. What could I say? Don't move? Don't go to school with him? Don't you dare like him because he's trouble?

But anything like that would hurt my friend and separate us more than the miles soon would.

"I always want you to be happy."

"Thanks, Wendy."

It didn't matter at all whether the note inside the jewelry box had been hers. Not at all.

More worried than ever about Jennifer, I returned home to find Alice and Gayle crashed on the floor in Alice's room. Both sweaty from their run.

I poked my head through the doorway. "Hey."

They looked at each other and then at me.

"Mind if I come in?"

"I don't mind." Gayle sat up and drew her legs into a crisscross.

Alice did the same.

"I'm sorry I couldn't run with you today."

They stared at me.

"Something's going on with Jen, and you know I still care about her."

"Of course." Gayle's voice was as soft as her eyes.

"Sure." Alice nodded.

"Well, I need your help with something."

Chapter 7

"We need a name, like a private investigation firm." Gayle was certainly getting into this surveillance thing.

Alice spewed her cola onto the school lawn. "I'm sorry." She wiped her mouth with the back of her hand and cleared her throat. "Why do we need a name?"

Ignoring the question, I grabbed both of Gayle's upper arms. "I think that's a great idea. Then we could use it as a sort of code when one of us hears something worth reporting."

"How about W.A.G.?" Gayle bounced her eyebrows.

"Like a dog's tail?" Alice pulled a tissue from her purse and wiped her skin. "It's cute."

Gayle laughed. "I didn't plan it like that. I just used the initials of our first names."

"Well, I love it. For both reasons." I placed my hand, palm down, in the space before us.

Gayle rested her hand on mine, and Alice topped them with hers.

"One, two, three, WAG!" we shouted, and released our hands into the air.

Lunchtime and the three of us took advantage of a table closer to Jennifer and the ballerinas.

"Oh, I forgot my napkin." Gayle spoke above the cafeteria roar and winked at me as she walked as near to our subject's table as possible.

I rolled my eyes. Subtle, Gayle. Real subtle.

She returned and sat across from Alice and me. "I heard something about this weekend."

"Like what?" I leaned toward Gayle and strained to hear.

Gayle lowered her voice to a whisper. "They were talking about Jennifer and her boyfriend, and Jennifer said, 'This might be the weekend.'"

I swallowed to keep my lunch from rising to my throat.

With Jen still on my mind, I opened the front door and let Melissa in the house for our Thursday session. As I'd agreed when she first approached me about tutoring, we never spoke about it at school after she accepted the deal. Eye contact was the most that passed between us, even in classes we had together.

"Did you get any more done?" Melissa glided into the foyer and pressed folded cash into my hand.

Me get more done? She had to be kidding. "No, it's your paper. I was hoping you'd work on it until we met again." I glanced behind me to be sure Mom hadn't seen the money transaction. Not that there was anything wrong with getting paid for tutoring. But I hadn't found the right time to talk to her about it.

"Well, I thought maybe you worked on it. I added some things and emailed the document back to you right before I left home. Didn't you see it?"

"Uh, no."

"Then we have a lot to do." She led the way to my room.

I followed at her heels like a servant. She sat on the end of my bed, and I sat in front of my computer. Waiting for the application to open the document she sent, I tucked the money into my nightstand drawer.

Back at the computer, I stared at Melissa's additions. What in the world? This couldn't have been written by someone in high school.

"Melissa, you know the program can check your spelling and grammar, right?" But that was the least of her problems.

She stood next to my chair. "Oh, I looked at that, but I didn't see anything wrong with the way I wrote it."

I turned my face away from her and rolled my eyes.

We coursed through the spelling and grammar check. With each stop—and there were many—I did my best to explain why the sentence needed to be corrected. Verb and subject didn't match. Incorrect possessive pronoun. Misplaced modifier. And the punctuation? Yikes!

Melissa took my place at the computer for a while so I could stretch and get us a snack. I returned, and she took a bathroom break. I filled in some gaps in content and corrected some of her corrections. We worked nonstop until someone rapped at my door.

Mom's voice reached us from the other side. "Wendy,

Melissa's mother is here."

Melissa and I glanced at each other and at the clock on the screen.

Rats! Already so late, and the paper due the next day. Both of our papers.

"I have to go, and I don't think I can finish this by myself." She opened her eyes wide.

For the first time, she was right. If this paper was going to be ready by morning, I'd have to be the one to finish it.

She blinked three times.

I sighed. "Okay. There's not much left to do." Yeah, not really. "I'll make the rest of the changes and email it to you."

"Thanks."

"Don't forget to print it out and take it to school."

"I won't."

My scalp tingled. This wasn't the ideal way to handle finishing the paper, but what choice did we have? She needed my help, and we'd run out of time.

After dinner, I put the final touches on my own history paper. Then I worked on Melissa's until, exhausted, I took a shower and climbed into bed.

My head hurt. But with each week tutoring Melissa, I'd be closer to my goal. It would be worth it.

With a sip of water, I swallowed an aspirin and crashed backward onto my pillow. I pictured Sam's and Mrs. V's faces when I got off the plane in Anchorage. Yes, it would be so worth it.

I fell asleep thinking about Alaska.

Chapter 8

As the teacher collected our papers Friday in world history class, I jiggled my knee under my desk.

Why did I feel like such a criminal? So what if I helped out another student by typing a few sentences. It wasn't like anyone would know.

Then why was our teacher looking at me so funny? I glanced sideways at Melissa. She stared straight ahead.

She wouldn't have told anybody, would she? Especially after making me keep the secret about tutoring her.

From the desk behind mine, David poked me in the back. "Hey, what's with you?"

I half-turned. "Nothing," I whispered. "I'll talk to you after class."

Later in the hall, David swung his long arm around my shoulders. "Everything okay?"

"Yeah, I'm just a little tired." And worried. If only I could talk to him about my dilemma. It would be nice to confide in someone. Extra nice to lean against his shoulder.

"Not too tired for tomorrow, I hope." He stroked my hair.

That energized me. "Of course not." I shifted my books higher in my arms. "What should I bring for the picnic?"

"What can you make?"

"Almost anything you can put between two slices of bread. How about egg salad?"

"That sounds good. I'll tell Ben to tell Carla." He glanced left and right and then kissed me on the forehead.

How could I worry about anything after that?

When Alice and I got off the bus after school, Papa D was home. "I'll take care of Adam and feed the dogs." He loosened the tie around his neck and unbuttoned his collar.

"You girls can get started on your run."

"Thanks!" Alice and I said, and we kissed his cheek.

Alice phoned Gayle as we parted to change our clothes and shoes.

Back in the kitchen in ten minutes, I strapped on a water bottle carrier. "Alice, where's yours?"

"I can't find it."

"I'll share my water with you."

"Thanks." Her blue eyes softened. "I'm glad you can run with us today."

I pulled my hair back into a ponytail and avoided her gaze. "Me too. I really do want to run with you and Gayle as much as possible."

"I didn't say anything before, but I've been wondering why you're spending so much time with Melissa. I mean, I understand you're tutoring her, but how can you afford that much time? And she must be really bad at writing."

"I can't afford not to. And yes, she really is bad." I shook my head and laughed. "Let's go."

I headed out the door before Alice could ask anything more.

Alice and I arrived at the park and immediately spotted Gayle stretching in her neon green running shorts. Gayle wasn't afraid to be noticed. She'd gone from nerdy eighth-grade brainiac with bad hair and glasses to tall and sleek athletic high-school goddess. Gayle could be the poster child for metamorphosis.

She placed one foot atop the back of a bench and bent forward until her head reached her shin.

Huffing and puffing, Alice and I trudged toward her.

"Hey, my dad dropped me off, so I need to warm up." She swapped legs and stretched the other one.

Judging from the deepened pink of Alice's face, she was warmed up plenty. I wiped sweat off my forehead with a palm and offered her my water.

She took a sip.

"Don't you need more?"

"I'm okay. Maybe later."

I gulped a quarter of the bottle.

Gayle twisted at the waist and then swung her arms in a semicircle. "Ready."

The three of us took off down a path beneath the oaks.

"This is nice for a change. And cooler than out in our neighborhood." I inhaled deeply, and my troubles drifted away on the exhale.

We ran without speaking until we neared another row of benches.

"Isn't that Mr. Stanley?" Alice directed her chin toward a bench in the shadows.

Gayle and I glanced in that direction.

His head tilted toward a book held in one hand, his glasses down low on his nose.

"Yeah, it is." After the way he'd treated me, I didn't care to speak to him. Maybe if I pretended I didn't see him—rats!

He glanced up at us before I could look away.

"Hi, Mr. Stanley." Alice and Gayle spoke at once.

He nodded at them in my peripheral vision.

I held my nose in the air and focused straight ahead on the path as I passed.

He'd been rude to me first, so why did I feel so rotten?

After the run, Alice and I walked toward home, both of us quiet for a time.

I hadn't shown it lately, but I truly was fortunate to have a sister, a little brother, and two parents at home. God never promised me a life free of problems when he brought the Rends into my world. As long as we stood together, any of us could handle whatever came our way. I glanced sideways.

Alice turned her head toward me. "I'm so glad both our parents have had job interviews. Dad seems more relaxed lately."

"I'm glad, too. Mom acts hopeful." I'd prayed for them both to find work. And not just for selfish reasons.

"Do you think one of them will get something soon?" Her expression begged me for reassurance that everything would be okay.

I had to give her that. Why not ease her mind if it didn't cost me anything? "I think so."

Her eyelids crinkled up, and the corners of her mouth drooped.

"Alice, are you worried about music camp or something else?"

She stopped walking. "It's just that—well, I don't want anything to change."

I stopped, too. "You mean with our family?"

She nodded with a brief double-jerk of her head.

"I don't either. Even though our money situation's changed, can't we promise each other nothing else will?"

She smiled. "Yeah."

We hugged. We were still in this together.

She wrenched herself free of me and opened her mouth wide, gasping. "You stink."

We doubled over laughing and laughed in fits the rest of the way home.

Alice's phone rang in her pocket as we walked into the house. From her smile and quickened step, I figured the caller to be my cousin Jerome.

"Hi …" She trailed to her room.

Growls from lack of an afternoon snack escaped my belly, and something smelled good coming from the kitchen. Meatloaf?

I poked my head through the doorway. Belle and Chanceaux flanked Papa D near the stove.

Adam sat at the counter doing homework and raised his head. "Hey, Wendy."

"Mmm, something smells like Mom's meatloaf." I stroked Adam's hair.

Papa D grinned like he was pleased with himself. "It is. She told me where she keeps her recipes, so I thought I'd surprise her."

"Isn't she home?" I gently moved Belle's mouth away from my leg to stop her from licking my perspiration.

"No. She had another interview. It was a good day for both of us." He peeked through the oven door at the meatloaf.

"I'm glad. Need any help?"

"No, thanks. I have the green beans going and the potatoes boiling." He pointed at each item. "She'll be home soon. I'll whip the potatoes and ask her if she'd rather have chives or garlic in them."

My mouth watered. "Okay. Can't wait. But I badly need a shower." I headed to my room. Belle and Chanceaux were smart enough to stay in the kitchen for a possible treat.

The water blasted my face in the shower as I scrubbed my scalp.

I ran fingers over the still-oily parts of my face and lathered them again with acne soap. Pimple-free was my goal for my picnic date with David.

Wow, I'd almost forgotten about the eggs. Right after dinner, I'd better boil some for the egg salad.

Rinsed and dried, I pulled on pajamas. I hadn't given a thought to what I'd wear to the picnic. I sure could use Jennifer's advice.

Jen. I missed her for so many reasons. The ultimate fashionista, she planned her outfits for each day way in advance. She was probably planning right now what she'd wear this weekend.

The blood rushed to my ears.

This weekend. What was it Gayle heard Jennifer say? *This might be the weekend.*

What exactly did that mean? I yanked a wide-toothed comb through my damp hair and shuddered. Jen wasn't planning to have—she couldn't be. With the first guy she liked? No.

Drugs? I shook my head. No way.

Neither of those would be like Jennifer. She was independent, clear-headed. A church-goer. And she wouldn't do anything that might jeopardize her future as a dancer.

Then what could it be? If I figured out the right way to ask her, maybe she would tell me.

My phone lay on the bed where I'd thrown it.

I reached for it but startled from a sudden knock on my door, my heart pounding.

"Yes?" My voice squeaked.

"Hi, sweetie. I wanted to let you know I was home, and dinner's ready."

"I'll be right there," I called through the wall.

I wrapped a robe over my pajamas and shoved my toes into a pair of flip-flops.

My call to Jennifer would have to wait.

Please, God, don't let the weekend she spoke of start tonight.

I let Jen's phone ring until I was sure it would go to voicemail.

She answered, breathless. "Wendy?"

She still had me in her contacts! "Yeah. Hey, Jen."

"Were we supposed to talk tonight? If so, I forgot. I have a date with Brian, and I'm running late."

If this was the weekend thing she and her friends had been talking about, I didn't have time to waste. "Brian?"

"The guy I'm seeing. Didn't I tell you his name?"

"No." But I knew exactly who he was, and finally I had his name.

"I'm really in a hurry." Clothes hangers clicked and clattered.

I bit my tongue to keep from saying, "Sorry I bothered you. We can talk later." I needed information, and I couldn't give up if Jennifer faced some sort of risk.

"What's up?" She growled, though I was sure it wasn't at me, and more hangers clacked.

"Nothing. Well, just, never mind. You like him a lot, huh?"

"Yeah." Her voice sounded like it did when she ate chocolate cheesecake. "He's a little older, a junior."

"Is that why you like him so much?"

"Well, no. I dunno. He treats me like I'm older too, you know?"

"Like how?"

She lowered her voice an octave. "When we've gone out, he's brought me a red rose each time. And tonight he's bringing a bottle of wine and two glasses in the car, so we can share a toast before we go out to dinner."

My teeth clamped together as I held back a groan. "Jen, you know that's against the law. And dangerous." Shoot. Now she'd be mad at me.

Her mild snort came through the phone line. "Don't worry. We'll only drink a little."

I stopped myself from commenting that a little was still wrong. I softened my voice and chose my words carefully. "Have you thought about why he's trying to get you to drink?

"No, but there's no reason. He's just more sophisticated than the boys we know. So what?"

"I don't think drinking makes him sophisticated."

"Why are you saying that? I finally found a boy I like, and I don't want to act like an infant in front of him."

"Jen, I'm sorry. I'm—I'm just worried, that's all. I don't want you to get into trouble." My mind raced with possible scenarios, one more horrible than the last. .

"I don't understand. Why are you getting all maternal on me?"

"I don't mean to. Just—please, Jen, don't drink tonight. Please?"

Silence.

"Promise me." Memories of eighth grade flooded my brain when I'd worried Jen might have an eating disorder. But as her one-and-only best friend back then, I'd had a right to demand a promise. Did I have a right to now?

"I can't promise. I have to think about it."

I waited, her silence deafening. "Are we still friends?"

She paused and took an audible breath. "Yes. Always. But I gotta go."

"Okay."

"'Bye, Wendy."

"'Bye, Jen." My hand jittered as I dropped the phone

onto my bed.

I pressed my clasped hands against my forehead. If he pushed her to drink, what else would he push her to do?

God, please don't let Brian change Jennifer in any way. Please keep her safe.

She stayed on my mind until I dozed off, lying on top of the bedspread.

I awoke to my Cajun music ringtone, unsure at first whether it was morning or night.

David. I cleared my throat and said hello.

"Hey, Wendy. Did you have a good run?"

"Yeah, I did, and I needed it."

"You sound tired, but if you keep it up, you'll be better off when the season starts."

"I know. What did you do this evening?"

"Baseball scrimmage. The jamboree is next Saturday. First game is the week after."

"Right. Sorry I forgot."

"That's okay. Can you meet me at the game? It's at home."

"I'm pretty sure I can as long as I can get a ride. What are the plans for the picnic tomorrow?"

"Ben and I will pick you up at noon after we get Carla."

"Okay. I'll have the egg salad sandwiches."

"Great. We'll take care of everything else. My mom made out a list." He snorted.

"Aww, she's so sweet."

"Yeah, I know. But I can't wait to see you without our parents around." His voice flowed smooth and low.

Warmth wrapped my heart while sparks shot through my extremities. "Me neither."

"Then I'll see you tomorrow. 'Night, Wendy."

"'Night, David."

If only I could lie on my back and replay his intoxicating words in my head, but thoughts of Jen poured into my brain.

And eggs waited to be boiled.

Chapter 9

With a bag of chilled egg salad sandwiches hanging from one hand, I clung to David with my other arm as soon as we stepped outside my door Saturday.

On the way to Ben's car, I pressed as close to David's side as I could and still allow us to walk. My swingy cotton skirt had little room to swing.

So what if I appeared clingy and somewhat needy? I needed David more than I'd ever thought I would need anyone. His warmth oozing through my skin and his scent filling the air I breathed rejuvenated and calmed me at the same time. Should I tell him how much I missed him?

"Wow, I really like this attention." He flashed a sparkling white smile as he looked at me sideways.

I squeezed tightly against his shoulder. "I hope we get to talk in private today." My voice came out more sultry than I'd intended.

"Yeah, me too!" His faced reddened.

I smiled at his enthusiasm and took a deep breath. In spite of what he might be thinking, it was time to tell him about Papa D, our money problems, the deal I'd made with Melissa, and—

"Hi, Wendy." Carla popped out of the front seat of Ben's car and pulled the seatback forward.

I let the air out of my lungs, handed David the bag, and climbed into the backseat.

"This is the perfect spot." I sighed, relaxing my back against the trunk of the shady oak tree. We'd chosen this spot for its distance from the more crowded picnic tables. An old quilt cushioned the four of us on the ground, cool despite the warm breeze. The aroma of spring grass was the smell of every happy day I'd ever known.

"What would you like to drink?" David held a diet soda in one hand and a bottle of water in the other.

"Water, please." I accepted the bottle and then a small

bag of potato chips from Carla.

"These are ham and cheese on whole wheat with mayo." Ben took sandwiches from a basket and set them on a towel, along with my egg salad on white bread.

"I'm impressed, Ben." I popped a chip into my mouth.

"Don't be." He grinned. "Our mom watched me every step of the way."

"I made spice cupcakes for dessert." Carla set a plastic container on the blanket.

"Cream cheese icing? Yum." I smiled at Carla.

David took a sip of his cola. "Wanna split one of each kind of sandwich?"

"Sure." I reached for a paper plate.

We all munched and chatted, surrounded by the sounds of birds and distant children's laughter.

Ben finished first and then stood and pulled Carla to her feet. "Carla and I are going for a walk. We'll see you a little later."

"Have fun," I said. How dorky did that sound?

Carla skipped off the blanket, giggling.

David and I looked at each other. He blushed, and heat rose to my cheeks.

I took a big swallow of water and patted my mouth with a paper napkin.

He shifted on the blanket to face me and edged closer. I tucked my skirt around my thighs and knees.

He leaned across the front of me, propping himself with an arm on my other side. He didn't waste a second but kissed me, soft and easy.

The thrill suspended me in the air like my first Ferris wheel ride.

He pulled back a few inches and looked at me as if to check and see if it was okay for him to continue.

We'd never had more than one kiss at a time before. But I nodded, and the weight of his second kiss pressed the back of my head against the tree bark.

I reached around his neck with both hands.

He reached behind my back and pulled me closer.

It was the longest kiss we'd ever had. Someone should've broken it, but I didn't want it to end.

He drew back and studied my face with an expression almost like—like he was in pain somehow. He swallowed hard and took his place next to me again, his back against the tree.

I inhaled a sharp breath, and my mouth stayed open as my mind struggled to return from the profoundness of that kiss.

He ran his fingers along my arm and said, "Did you

want to talk to me about something?"

Yes, what was it? What had I wanted to talk about? Oh, right. "Yeah, there's some stuff I'm worried about."

He faced forward but kept close to my side. "Go ahead. Talk to me."

I leaned my head against his shoulder and spilled my guts about all the things troubling me.

He caressed my face. "I think everything's gonna be okay."

"You do?"

"Sure. Your Mom and Papa D won't both be without jobs for long. Your family will have money again." He glanced away. "And you'll get to go to Alaska."

My heart melted like the icing on the cupcakes waiting to be eaten. It was hard for him to think of my seeing Sam again. But I couldn't imagine feeling about Sam the way I had begun to feel about David. I just didn't think I needed to say it. We'd agreed we wouldn't discuss my friendship with Sam.

David squeezed my hand. "I wish I could convince you not to worry so much about Jennifer."

"Because she can take care of herself?"

"Uh-huh. Just like you can. Neither one of you is a pushover."

"I suppose if she were worried about me starting to drink, I'd tell her I could take care of myself."

"Worrying just wears you out. And as long as you're tutoring Melissa, you'll be tired enough."

"I know. I do that a lot—take on more than I can handle."

"Yet you always manage to handle it." He stroked my hair.

"True. But I practically had to write Melissa's paper for her. I don't feel good about that."

"Do you think you did anything wrong?"

"I don't know. I don't think so. Well, I do worry about the teacher finding out about it."

"I can understand that, but teachers help us a lot sometimes. You know, giving us hints about how to work through a problem or word something the right way."

He so knew how to make me feel better. I didn't ever want to be without him.

He kissed me gently again on the lips. "Plus, maybe she'll get better at writing."

"Maybe she will," I whispered a fraction of an inch from his lips, and then I kissed him.

A cough broke the spell.

"Hey, kids." Carla grinned with her tongue against her

white teeth.

Ben bounced his eyebrows at David.

David pushed himself off the blanket.

"Feel like trying out the swings?" Carla tossed her hair. "They're not far."

"Okay." I drew my legs to the side and prepared to stand.

David offered me his hand and helped me up.

Together the four of us made our way leisurely down a path toward the playground.

I halted in mid-stride. "I don't believe it. Does he live at this park?" I said under my breath.

David turned around. "Why did you stop?"

Ben and Carla glanced at me, then each other, and kept walking.

"Look past those trees. Mr. Stanley is over there—again. He was at the park yesterday when Alice and I met Gayle for our run."

"Good. We can go over there, and you'll see he must've had something on his mind last time you tried to talk to him. He didn't mean to be rude."

"Are you serious?"

"Yes." David took my hand and led me toward Mr. Stanley.

We maneuvered a shallow ditch and arrived in front of him.

"Well, hello again, Wendy. David." He nodded at each of us. "Good to see you both. What brings you to the park?"

I pinched David's arm, and he spoke first. "Hi, Mr. Stanley. We're here for a picnic with my brother and his girlfriend."

"That's nice." He gave us a relaxed smile.

I skipped the compulsory hello. "We were about to go on the swings."

"Sounds like fun." He laughed. "I might try reliving my youth."

My manners returned in spite of myself. "How are you doing? Still teaching at Bellingrath?"

"Yes, but it's not quite the same as it was."

"How's that?"

"Some people we both knew are gone. Mrs. Perez isn't there any longer." The sparkle vanished from his eyes.

"Really?" I sat on the bench at the opposite end. "She was also one of my favorite teachers." I placed a hand to my warming cheek, not meaning to indirectly compliment him as I had complimented her.

"Is she teaching somewhere else?" David asked.

"She moved to another town and is teaching there."

"I'm sorry." That was dumb. Sorry for what? For her maybe getting a better job, or …

Wow. He looked like he'd lost his best friend. Had he? Maybe he missed Mrs. Perez as badly as I missed Jennifer. He and Mrs. Perez were together a lot at Bellingrath, even working as a kind of tag team to keep us kids under control. I always thought she was married, but the title "Mrs." didn't prove anything. I searched my memory, waiting for an image of a ring on her hand to pop up in my mind's eye. Nothing appeared.

And how many actual friends did Mr. Stanley have? He was so … eccentric in the way he dressed and behaved. Is that why he was alone at the park so much?

Patterns of sunlight and shadow danced on his face. I couldn't read anything in his expression.

"Well, I hope she's happy where she is. If you talk to her, please tell her hello for me."

"Me too," David said.

"I will. We'll probably write to each other. I'll let you know how she's doing when I run into you again."

"Thanks, Mr. Stanley." I stood and straightened my skirt, preparing to leave.

As if he didn't want me to go, he slapped the bench seat with an open palm. "What have you been up to,

Wendy?"

How lonely was he if he wanted two teenagers to stay and talk to him? I exchanged a glance with David and sat down again.

And as for what I had been up to, so much had happened I wasn't sure where to start. Items of public knowledge seemed a good place. "My mom married Alice's dad, so I'm part of a big family now."

"Wonderful. Are you still writing and drawing?"

"Sometimes. I started tutoring someone in English composition."

Mr. Stanley raised his eyebrows and peered over his glasses like he did in eighth-grade English class. "Interesting. How's that going?"

I took a deep breath. "It's not easy."

"No, it's not."

The difficulty of his profession sunk in. How patient he must have had to be with us.

"If you get stuck or need any advice, you could email me."

"Oh. That's awfully nice of you. Thanks." I pulled out my phone and created a contact for him. He gave me his email address.

"I hope high school is good to you both and to Alice,

too." He crossed his legs and clasped his knee.

"It's pretty good so far."

David reached for my hand. "We'd better get going before my brother wonders what happened to us."

"Yeah, we'd better. Thanks, Mr. Stanley."

"Of course. I meant what I said, Wendy. Let me know if you need any help."

"Thank you, I will. See you later." I turned on my heels.

David and I strode out of earshot.

"See? Told you." David squeezed me around the waist.

I sighed and shook my head. "When you're right, you're right."

Mr. Stanley had probably been tired, or maybe just lonely, wishing for an adult friend when he was in the park after the parade—or he may have been looking for one.

The note in the jewelry box. Mrs. Perez's journal! The one she wrote in each morning during the last semester of eighth grade. Lined paper in mixed colors, including that particular shade of blue. Sky blue.

Too bad I couldn't remember what her handwriting looked like. Or Mr. Stanley's either.

"David, did I ever tell you what was inside the jewelry

box I bought at the flea market?"

I waited all night for a call from Jennifer. Not that she'd said she would call. Or would need to. Her ballerina friends would be more than happy to hear about her date with Brian. But I was the one who'd known her the longest—and the best.

Chapter 10

After church Sunday, the family gathered in the kitchen over a box of glazed donuts. I was on my third. Anyone who says sweetness can't be smelled hasn't inhaled the aroma of a donut.

Mom had thawed one of her crawfish pies and popped it into the oven for lunch.

"Wendy and Alice, we've been thinking." Papa D had a serious look, his brow furrowed.

I held my breath. *Please, not the allowances.*

Alice and I exchanged wide-eyed glances. I slumped on my stool.

"We think we should invite David and Jerome to have dinner with us," Mom announced.

I perked up, back straight and toes on the stool rung. "Really?"

"When?" Alice slid her hands along the countertop toward our parents and leaned on her elbows.

"As soon as we can plan something convenient for everyone. Check with the boys for a weekend when they're both available." Mom smiled like she was pleased with herself over our enthusiasm. Did she expect anything different?

Alice's face shone like somebody turned on her lightbulb. She hadn't seen Jerome since he drove up from Bayou Calmon on New Year's Day.

"What made you decide to do that?" I wouldn't have to figure out a way to pay back David and his family on my own for the invitations they'd extended to me. And my allowance seemed safe, at least for the time being.

"David's family has been so nice to invite you to do things with them. We thought we should return the favor. And Alice hasn't seen Jerome in a while. We want the boys to know they're welcome here."

"Thank you!" Alice and I shouted.

Alice ran to Papa D and hugged him.

I jumped off the stool and hugged Mom.

"We may be on a tight budget, but we can share what

we have," Papa D said, his sentence broken into fragments from Alice's continued squeezing of his chest.

"Think about whether you'd like a casual or formal dinner and what you'd like for us to make." Mom patted my back. "Within reason."

"Can we go ahead and call the boys to see when they can make it?" I released Mom.

"Of course. The hardest part might be getting them here at the same time."

Alice and I tore out of the kitchen toward our rooms.

Planning this dinner was just the thing to get my mind off Jennifer.

Chapter 11

Jennifer sprinted toward my bus as soon as it arrived at school Monday morning.

Unusual, but was it a good sign or a bad one? I squinted to read her face and got nothing.

She was waiting below when I came down the steps.

"Wendy, I need to talk to you," she whispered, glancing behind her.

"Sure, Jen." I walked toward a less crowded area of the lawn instead of toward the building. She followed next to me.

This was what people meant when they said they were afraid to know something but afraid not to.

She hopped in front of me, and I almost ran into her. "I'm glad you called me Friday before my date. I thought about what you said the whole time I was getting ready to go out."

I scanned the freckles across her nose. "You did?"

"Yeah, and I thought about all the things that could go wrong if I drank with Brian." She paused. "So I didn't."

I sighed, fear releasing from my chest.

"I'm not saying I'll never drink."

"I understand." But at least she might not start before the end of ninth grade.

"It's just, well, there are so many things more important to me right now than that."

I hugged her. "That's what I hoped you'd realize. How'd he take it when you refused?"

She tilted her head from side to side, her mouth twisted. "He wasn't happy."

"I figured. Are you still seeing each other?"

"Yeah, but he'd better get used to the fact that I'm not the type to be pushed into anything."

"Absolutely." I smiled with my lips closed tight, my insides jumping for joy.

She cocked an eyebrow. "So we'll see how he handles it."

I laughed. Brian probably never met the likes of Jennifer before.

She trotted away a few yards and stopped. "I forgot! Here're your tickets to my dance recital." She rushed back to me and pulled them from her purse.

I grinned and held out my hand. "Thank you."

"I can't wait to see you and David there." She tapped my arm and sped away again.

That was the Jen I knew, and she left me with a lighter heart. She may not always live close enough for me to know what would happen to her in the future, but while she was still around, somebody like Brian would meet with resistance from both of us.

"Melissa must've gotten a good grade." David imitated the squeals and rapid hand movements of the Sticks as we walked out of history class.

"She should've," I whispered, my head low.

"If you're that good, maybe I should hire you to tutor me," he said under his breath. "Priii-vate-ly."

I soft-punched him in the belly. "That's not even funny. I hope we don't get any more writing assignments other than for English class before school ends."

"Aww, my baby's tired." He cupped the back of my neck with one hand. "And grouchy."

"David!" I tried to grab him, but he leapt out of reach, and I snatched a handful of air.

He returned to my side with his lips pouted.

I flipped hair off my neck with one hand. "I really am tired, and I don't know if I can make enough money to go to Alaska no matter how hard I try. Plus, what about Alice?"

He squinted and glanced to his left. "What about her?"

Obviously, he was trying to remember if I'd told him anything about Alice that he was already supposed to know.

"She had her heart set on going to a music camp in Texas this summer. Am I supposed to leave her?"

"I don't know. I never heard of such a thing as music camp."

"Trust me. It's a thing. She doesn't have time to make extra money because she has to watch Adam while I tutor and Mom and Papa D go on job interviews."

David shrugged.

"She's taken care of Adam for years. Doesn't she deserve to go?" My voice grew unintentionally loud.

David's eyes widened. People turned and stared.

"Sorry. I'm not mad at you." I rubbed his arm.

He patted my hand remaining on his arm. "I wish I knew how to solve your problem." He pressed his lips together and squinted again.

"It's okay. Just talking to you helps. Thanks."

"Glad I'm not totally useless." He lifted my chin using his thumb and forefinger.

I smiled from his affectionate touch. "How do you feel about a girl asking a boy out on a date? Besides dinner at my house."

His face brightened. "If it's you, I'm all for it."

"Well, you might want to hear the reason before you agree." I tilted my head.

He laughed. "I'm sure I can handle it."

"It's for Jennifer's dance recital. She gave me two tickets." I produced them from my purse.

"I'm still not scared." He glanced at the date and time.

"It's a dressy affair." I raised my eyebrows.

"No problem. I'll dust off my coat and tie." He grinned.

I kissed his cheek. "Talk to you later then. Gotta get to class."

And carve out time for the recital from my schedule.

Melissa phoned me right after I got home from school. What did she want now? I needed a day off.

I sighed and answered. "Hello?"

"How would you like to make some extra money?"

Seriously, she had a future as a telemarketer.

"Well?"

If it involved more time with Melissa, I wasn't interested. "I am making extra money."

"Besides what you're making from me."

"What are you talking about?" I was in no mood for guessing games.

"A few of my friends could use some help with their writing, too."

I paused. An opportunity to make more money for Alaska? Doing what I was already doing. But how could I take on more work?

"I don't have many afternoons available to meet with anybody else."

Melissa huffed like I was ridiculously difficult. Or stupid. "Can't you communicate by email or phone and work over the Internet?"

"Mayyy-be. Sometimes." My thoughts wandered to Alice. What if I could make enough money for her, too?

"What's your answer? My friends are waiting for me to call them back." Melissa's words cut through the airwaves.

"Wait. Who are these people?" I didn't appreciate being rushed.

"I'll text you their names and phone numbers. They'll expect to hear from you tonight."

Wow, I must seem pretty desperate for money for Melissa to be so sure I'd agree.

I glanced at my clothes and shoes. They didn't appear old or worn like I was nouveau-poor. I faced myself in the mirror.

My sunken eyes held no energy, no sparkle, and little hope. They told the story of a girl ready to try just about anything to get what she wanted.

The extra work was killing me, but the money rolled in.

My new clients and I communicated by email, passing documents back and forth through cyberspace. When I noticed small things like punctuation or spelling that needed correcting, I corrected them. If a phrase or sentence could be worded in a better way, I coached them on what to do. If they couldn't grasp the concept, I simply made the changes myself and sent the docs back to my clients for approval. And they always approved. Why wouldn't they since I made their lives easier?

When I ran into a question my reference books didn't answer clearly enough for me, I emailed Mr. Stanley. He always saved me.

The word got around among Melissa's friends. Every few days, someone new contacted me, begging for assistance. I added them to my client list and calculated my future earnings.

Everyone's grades improved, but I struggled to stay awake in class and maintain mine.

Chapter 12

Friday night for Jen's dance recital, I patted concealer on dark circles under my eyes and applied liquid foundation to the rest of my pasty skin. Extreme computer use, no time for myself, and diminished sleep had taken its toll on my appearance.

A new dress lay on my bed, the first one this year. I'd saved all my allowance since Papa D lost his job, and it seemed only right to spend some of it to look nice for Jen's recital. At least it would serve as an Easter dress, too. I snipped the price tag, marked down twenty-five percent.

As I dressed, I prayed I could make it until the end of the school year without collapsing from fatigue. I hadn't been able to run with Alice and Gayle but only managed to fit in the training required by my track coach—and forced myself to do that. Track meets hadn't even started yet.

Fully dressed, with loosely curled hair cascading over my shoulders, I trudged to the living room.

"Wendy, you look so pretty." Alice held up her phone and snapped a photo before I could stop her.

"Thank you." I gave her a tiny smile. "I'm sorry you don't get to dress up and go out much." I didn't even think about asking her to go with me. It was always David.

"It's okay." She shook her head. "Don't worry about me. I'd go on a date if someone I liked better than Jerome would ask me out."

That wasn't likely to happen, and we both knew it.

The doorbell rang.

"'Bye, Mom." I directed my voice toward the kitchen. "See you later."

"Have fun!" Mom and Papa D called out.

David stood on the front porch, spectacular in his coat and tie. He illuminated my existence.

"Hey, beautiful." His eyebrows squeezed together above his nose. "How're you feeling?"

I stood on tiptoe and kissed his lips for caring. "I'm good. I'm with you."

He squeezed my waist. "Ben's going to drop us off and go out with some of his friends. I'll call him to come get us afterward."

"Okay. I might try to catch Jennifer and talk to her before we leave." I slipped my hand into his.

"No problem." He led me to the car, and we climbed into the backseat.

I sat in awe of the stage and dancers, studying the lighting and the way it interacted with tulle costumes and glittery headdresses. David watched the stage intently, and my concern over his being bored evaporated.

My lips curled up at the corners. Even if he enjoyed watching a bunch of pretty girls dance around, I didn't care.

Jennifer entered the stage like a shining star, glorious and beautiful. How different tonight was from the spring program in eighth grade when I let jealous, spiteful feelings toward her consume me. Jen was my friend, tried and true, and I loved her as much as ever.

The performance ended, and we tried to make our way toward the stage, but body traffic flowed against us. We stepped into one of the rows and out of the way.

"What should I do, David? Should I try to get back there?"

"I dunno. Maybe you could call or text her to see if she can come out and meet you."

"Yes, that would be better." I found her in my contacts and selected her number. It rang and went to voice mail.

"No luck?"

"It's probably too noisy for her to hear the phone ring. I'll try texting."

I waited. Still no Jennifer.

The crowd cleared enough for us to zip to the stage.

I got the attention of a pair of adults standing near the backstage entrance. "Mind if I go in?"

"That's fine, but most of the dancers have gone, if you're looking for someone."

I took a chance Jennifer might have hung around, but there was no sign of her. I wanted so badly to see her, like old times.

I returned to David, disappointed. "You may as well call Ben to pick us up."

"I'm sorry you didn't find her."

"If I don't reach her tonight, I'll call her tomorrow." I kissed his cheek. "Thanks for waiting."

In a few minutes, we were in Ben's car on the way

home.

"I'm so glad you could go with me tonight." I snuggled against David.

"I was happy to," he whispered. Then he shouted at Ben, "Don't tell anybody I went to a ballet."

"Oh!" I slapped David's arm.

We pulled up to my house. The garage lights were on instead of the front porch light, which gave us more subtle light at the front door. Thank you to whoever did that, even if by mistake.

We reached the door, and David wrapped his arms around me, a full embrace unlike any I'd received before. We understood each other—and that a kiss was both welcomed and inevitable. I melted against him.

The front door flew open. David and I separated in a split second.

Mom!

"Wendy, something terrible has happened. Please come inside. You too, David."

We rushed into the foyer, and Mom closed the door behind us.

She took a deep breath. "Jennifer was in a car accident." She held fingers to her lips.

I gasped, my hand to my mouth.

"She's in the hospital. I'm so sorry, sweetie."

"No!"

Mom tried to hug me, but I bent and moaned like I'd taken a baseball to the belly.

David grabbed my shoulders and steadied me. "Mrs. Rend, do you know what happened?"

"No. I just got a call from Claire, Jennifer's mother. She and Mr. Sampson were at the hospital and wanted us to know."

Panic wrung my senses until I couldn't see, couldn't hear, couldn't feel David's touch. Jennifer had to be alive. She just had to be, and I had to see her.

"Mom, can we go please? *Now? Please?*" Uncontrollable tears drenched my cheeks and reached my neck. Mom's face blurred before me.

David handed me his handkerchief.

"Yes, honey, of course. But we need to tell Daniel and Alice first." She grabbed some tissues as she spoke, her face contorted as if she suffered seeing me in emotional pain.

I swallowed, wiped my face with David's handkerchief, and handed it back to him.

"David, you're welcome to ride with us. I can take you home later." Mom handed me the tissues, and I blew my

nose

"Thanks. I'll let my brother know."

I ran to Alice's room and burst in without knocking. Her eyes flew open wide. She sat on her bed, watching TV in her pajamas.

"Jen was in a bad wreck."

"Oh, no." She leapt off the bed and stumbled over her slippers. "Was that you screaming? I thought it was the TV in the living room."

I clutched her hands. "Mom can take us to the hospital. We need to go. Now."

"Okay, just give me a minute to change."

I returned to the living room where David waited. He'd removed his coat and tie, and his brow wrinkled when he saw me. "You're hyperventilating. Let's get a glass of water." He motioned me to the kitchen.

"Drink." He handed me a glass of tap water.

I drank, and my breathing slowed.

Alice appeared, along with Mom. "Let's go," Mom said.

We loaded into her car and sped backward down the driveway.

The four of us blasted into the hospital like gangsters.

Mom spoke to the lady at the front desk. "A friend of mine asked me to come. Her daughter was admitted. A car accident."

"Name?"

"Jennifer Sampson. She's fifteen."

I sobbed. Alice and David squeezed my hands from opposite sides. Tears trickled from the corners of Alice's eyes.

We dashed to the elevators.

The doors opened, and Mom said, "There's Jennifer's mother."

We hurried to her.

"Claire." Mom reached for Mrs. Sampson, and they hung onto each other.

"Cathy, Wendy, thank you for coming. Jennifer's grandparents are still on their way. My husband's picking them up."

"What have the doctors told you?" The women broke their embrace, and Mom held Mrs. Sampson at arms' length.

"Nothing. She's still in surgery." Mrs. Sampson reminded me of a worn-out doll, barely held together.

"There were head and back injuries. We don't know yet how bad."

"I'm so sorry." Mom sighed and shook her head. "Let's pray together." She motioned for Mr. Sampson's hand. Alice, David, and I joined them in the circle.

I raised my head at the end of the prayer, and red flashed in my vision.

Brian sat against the wall, his hands bandaged, a scrape across his cheek.

"There he is. That's him. He did this to Jennifer," I whispered to David and Alice.

We got home, and I called Gayle. Crying, I asked her to pray with me for Jennifer.

It was a long night, and I awoke every hour, hoping Jennifer's accident had been a terrible nightmare. Each time reality returned, my stomach pitched like one of David's fastballs.

At dawn, I gave up and took a shower and dressed.

Mom and Papa D sat in the kitchen having coffee.

"Couldn't sleep?" Papa D pressed his lips together and crinkled his eyes.

"Hardly." If I looked exhausted yesterday, I must appear zombie-like this morning. "Is there any news about Jen?"

"It's too soon, sweetie." Mom got up and kissed the top of my head.

Figured, but an ache squeezed my heart. I rubbed my face with both hands.

"Would you like some coffee with milk and sugar? It might make you feel better."

"Sounds good. Thanks."

She mixed it and handed me a mug.

I took a sip and looked them both in the eyes. "Did Jennifer's mom or dad say anything about the accident? I mean, how it happened?"

Mom and Papa D exchanged glances.

Mom stared into her cup. "The police determined that the boy driving Jennifer caused the accident," she said, her voice low.

"I knew it!" I slammed my hand on the counter, and my mug sloshed.

"But the boy's blood alcohol content was below the limit, even for an underage drinker," Papa D said. "And there was no alcohol in the car."

"So he won't even get into trouble, will he? What if

Jen—what if she dies?" I blubbered into my coffee-milk.

"It's up to his parents to decide his punishment." Mom reached for my hand. "And we're just going to continue to pray for Jennifer."

The pitch of my voice rose. "He's putting her in risky situations, you know?" I sniffed and wiped my nose with a paper napkin. "He's reckless, and he doesn't care about Jen like her friends do."

"We know. And I'm sure Jennifer's parents are going to talk to her about him."

The obvious question whether Mr. and Mrs. Sampson would get that chance hung in the air between us for a moment.

I slowly shook my head, the sweet drink turning sour in my mouth. "I hate him. I hate him so much." I kept my head down and stalked from the room.

Chapter 13

In spite of worrying about Jennifer that weekend, I had to fulfill my obligations to the students who'd hired me. And maybe that was for the best, because it kept my mind off the worst-case scenario for her. Mom hadn't heard any news from Mrs. Sampson, and Mom wouldn't let anyone call Jen's house or the hospital.

As many times as I asked for Mr. Stanley's advice, I never pried into whether he and Mrs. Perez remained in communication or had exchanged a note that could've wound up in the jewelry box I purchased. And he didn't pry into how many students I might be tutoring. Maybe he guessed that the questions I asked were for more than only myself and one other student. Maybe he didn't.

I did explain why I was tutoring. I'd never heard Mr. Stanley accused of being a gossip, so I figured the information was safe with him.

Email reply from him: I ADMIRE WHAT YOU'RE DOING, WENDY.

Guilt pinched me, and I rubbed my arms.

My reply: WELL, IT'S NOT TO SUPPORT THE FAMILY OR ANYTHING NOBLE LIKE THAT. I JUST WOULD LIKE FOR ALICE AND ME TO BE ABLE TO KEEP OUR SUMMER PLANS.

That was true. Since earning more per week than I could have ever dreamed, I wanted to help Alice reach her goal, too.

His reply: DON'T SELL YOURSELF SHORT. YOU'RE SHOWING INITIATIVE.

My reply: THANK YOU, MR. STANLEY. I'D BETTER GET BACK TO WORK.

He must've been lonely to have nothing better to do than help me. I hoped Mrs. Perez called or at least emailed him.

Sunday morning, a headache split my brain like a

worn-out wooden bat. But I dragged myself out of bed and got ready for church. It was one thing to pray hard at home like I'd been praying for Jennifer's recovery. It was another to go to God's house and beg Him. How could He ignore me then?

The five of us Rends rode quietly in Papa D's car. Adam squeezed between Alice and me, but he must've understood my mood because he didn't squirm or make noise.

"Everybody, please remember to pray for Jen," I spoke above a whisper but not by much.

"Absolutely," Papa D said.

Mom reached behind her seat, and we locked fingers for a few seconds.

Alice pouched her lower lip, nodded, and rubbed my shoulder.

"Mom, have you talked to Mrs. Sampson?"

"No, I didn't want to disturb her in case she was able to get some sleep."

"Do you think we can find out today how Jen's doing?"

"I'll call Claire this afternoon."

I stared out the window.

"Wendy, I know how much you love Jen, but I want

you to prepare yourself. Just in case—well, we must accept God's will no matter what happens."

My throat tightened. "I know." I choked out the words. *Please don't let Jen's death be in Your plan, God.*

Jennifer's image popped into my head every few minutes as I undressed after church, like she was nagging me to do something.

Mr. Stanley had taught Jen, too. If he'd heard about her accident …

I typed a short email to him.

MR. STANLEY,

SORRY TO BOTHER YOU WITH ANOTHER TOPIC, BUT MY FRIEND JENNIFER WAS IN A CAR ACCIDENT. DO YOU REMEMBER HER?

His reply came quickly.

YES, I DO REMEMBER JENNIFER, AND YOU'RE NOT BOTHERING ME. I READ ABOUT THE ACCIDENT IN THE NEWSPAPER BUT DIDN'T KNOW IF YOU WANTED TO TALK ABOUT IT. I'M SO SORRY, AND I'M PRAYING SHE'LL RECOVER SOON. PLEASE LET ME KNOW IF YOU HEAR ANYTHING FURTHER ABOUT HER.

I wasn't sure how to respond just then without crying. So I didn't.

Mom's phone rang as she, Alice, and I sat on the sofa and searched for a chick-flick to take our minds off things. She took the call and headed toward the garage. The way her voice trailed soft and low on the way, the caller had to be Mrs. Sampson.

Dread crept along my skin. Alice and I exchanged a knowing look.

Mom returned in a couple minutes and took a deep breath. Alice and I stared at her, our eyes unblinking.

"There's no change." She spoke calmly. "Jen is still in critical care."

I clung to the tiny shred of hope. "But that's a good thing, right? She hasn't gotten any worse." I pictured Saint Gemma, my confirmation namesake. She'd suffered terrible pain in her head and spine as a girl. If only Jen could have Gemma's will to survive.

"I think we should look at it that way. And keep praying, of course."

Mom knelt in front of Alice and me at the sofa. We

joined hands and bowed our heads.

Later in the evening, Alice heard back from Jerome about our dinner date for four. He could travel over from Bayou Calmon next Saturday. David had already let me know he was available, too.

I had forgotten about the dinner and didn't get excited like I would have before Jennifer's accident.

"Mom, is it a good time to go through with our plans?" I spoke to her in the privacy of her bedroom, not wanting to upset Alice by the question.

She paused in the middle of folding a shirt on her bed. "I think we need something normal in our lives right now, don't you?"

I shrugged. "I suppose so."

"And Alice would be so disappointed if we made her cancel with Jerome."

"True. It would break her heart."

"Look at it this way. We still need to cook and eat dinners, go to school, get jobs. We can and will continue to pray for Jennifer. We won't do her any good by stopping everything else."

"But if she gets well enough for us to visit her—"

"We'll make the time to go. Don't worry." Mom laid the folded shirt aside and patted my shoulder.

I'd drop everything if Mrs. Sampson called us with good news.

Mom crossed her arms. "Wendy, you've been spending most of your time in your room lately. Is that because of Jennifer, or is something else troubling you?"

My eyes held Mom's for a second. I took a deep breath. "You know how I've been helping Melissa every week?"

"Yes. You're helping her write a paper, aren't you?"

"I am. More than one. But I'm getting paid for it."

Her eyebrows shot up. "Why didn't you tell me?"

"I planned to, but you and Papa D were busy looking for work and going on interviews."

"That's no excuse. You can come to me any time I'm home and talk to me."

"I know. I stayed busy with Melissa and going out with David, and I started running again, and then …"

"Then what?"

"More people starting asking for my help with their papers, and now I don't have any free time."

"Are you getting paid by everyone?"

I nodded.

"How are you doing this? I've seen only Melissa here."

"We work over the Internet and by phone."

Her eyes clouded. "I'm sorry you feel that you have to make a living for yourself because your parents can't."

"Mom, that's not it at all. You and Papa D give me what I need. I just want to earn money for Alice and me to be able to take our trips this summer."

"I see." Her head down, she glanced up at me.

"What's wrong?"

"I hadn't thought about you going to Alaska by yourself."

"Well, please don't rule that out. Alice would go away by herself to music camp, right?"

"True, although that's not nearly as far." She uncrossed her arms. "But okay. I'll think about it."

"Thanks, Mom." I hugged her and turned toward the door.

"Wendy, exactly what kind of help are you giving your classmates? I mean, you're not simply writing the papers for them, are you?"

I pondered the question. No one just dumped a topic on me and had me write the paper. That would be cheating.

Or plagiarism? My clients did the research and emailed me their typed notes. I roughly arranged them and made suggestions about what they needed to fill in. They sent the document back to me and I edited it. Some more extensively than others, but I edited what they had.

I confidently answered, "No, Mom."

"That's a relief." She sighed and hugged me. "I love you, Wendy."

"I love you, too, Mom."

Chapter 14

A student worker from the school office walked into my Algebra class and handed the teacher a note.

I went back to working a problem at my desk.

"Wendy Robichaud?"

I raised my head.

"You're wanted in the office. Take your belongings."

Every head in the class turned my way.

My cheeks heated as I stood. Possible reasons for the summons stirred in my mind like a big pot of jambalaya but left a metallic taste in my mouth. I bent and gathered my purse and books, letting my hair fall to camouflage my face.

As I darted past Gayle and toward the exit, she mouthed *What*? I didn't stop, but raced down the halls toward the office and shouldered the glass door open.

"Mom?" She and Alice stood at the counter.

Acid rose in my esophagus. Something bad must've happened.

But Mom and Alice spun around and smiled.

"Good news, Wendy. Jennifer's awake, and I'm taking you to see her."

In the car, I texted David and told him I was leaving to see Jen. He didn't text back immediately, so he must've been in class.

Mom, Alice, and I stopped at a grocery store on the way to the hospital. I ran in and purchased one of those wrapped flower bouquets in spring colors.

Jennifer had been moved out of critical care and into a new room. That was something to celebrate.

"Prepare yourselves," Mom said to Alice and me. "Her mother said her face is stitched up and rather bruised."

Although visiting hours were in progress, Mom tapped lightly on the swinging door to Jennifer's room.

A nurse in colorful printed scrubs exited. "You can go in."

Mom pushed the door slowly, and Alice and I followed her with baby steps.

Mrs. Sampson sat at Jen's bedside, speaking to her in soft tones. She looked up and smiled.

Mom said, "Hi-iii," in a two-note singsong. "Look who's here to see you, Jennifer."

My eyes adjusted to the darkened room. Flat on her back, Jennifer turned her head toward me and smiled a lopsided smile.

I choked back a scream.

Nothing could've prepared me for Jennifer's face. One eye was swollen shut and surrounded by stitches. That half of her face, bigger than the other, wore a huge multi-colored bruise.

I stood with my mouth open for a few seconds. Mom rubbed my upper arm, bringing me back to coherence, and I swallowed.

"Hi, Jen. I'm so glad you're feeling better." My voice came out weak and shaky. I stepped nearer to her bed and offered her the bouquet. She was even harder to look at up close.

"It's a shock, right? But I'm in better shape than I

look." Her speech was slurred but the tone cheerful.

The covers reached up to her neck, and I shuddered to think of the condition of her body hidden underneath. Her hands lay exposed, an intravenous fluid feeding into one of them.

Mrs. Sampson chuckled. "Pain killers help her feel good, but she might get sleepy very soon."

"Thank you for the flowers." Jennifer took the bouquet with her free hand. She sniffed the blooms and handed the bouquet to her mother, exposing a bandaged forearm.

At least she could move.

"We've missed you." Alice edged closer to the bed.

"Thanks. I've missed both of you, too." Jennifer rested the back of her head on the pillow again.

Mrs. Sampson placed the flowers in a water pitcher. "Cathy, would you like to step out for a minute and have a cup of coffee with me?"

"Certainly." Mom followed her out of the room.

I sat in the chair closest to the bed, and Alice took the remaining seat. With time to adjust to Jen's appearance, I recognized her open eye as less than fully focused. "Are you getting tired, Jen?"

"No, I'm okay." She blinked the eye slowly. "You know what I was just thinking about?"

"What?" I leaned closer.

"The time you and I visited Tookie in the hospital when she had anorexia." Her tongue thickened on the last word.

"Yeah, I remember."

"It was hard to look at her. I never thought I'd be in the same spot." Her open eye teared up and dribbled from the outer corner.

I reached for a tissue. "May I dab the corner of your eye?"

"Yes."

"When can you come back to school?" Alice blurted.

I smiled at her in gratitude for changing the subject.

Jennifer rubbed her blanket between her fingers. "Maybe in time to see everyone before the semester ends. Mom's gonna get my assignments and take off from work to help me keep up with my classes."

"Great, Jen. I know you can do it. I'll pray you don't have to go to summer school as soon as you move."

"Oh. That's another thing." She tried to adjust her body, moaned, and then sighed. "We're not moving, at least not yet. Dad decided to commute for a year while I recuperate."

"Jen, I'm so glad. We can start tenth grade together."

I popped out of my chair, leaned over her bed, and gently cupped my hands around her shoulders in a sort of hug.

"Me too. But I'll have physical therapy to do. The doctor said for six months."

"I'll help you in whatever way I can if you need me."

"So will I," Alice said.

"Thank you. Who knows? Maybe I'll dance again by next year." She gave us a brave, lopsided grin.

"Of course you will." It would kill her not to dance again. *Please, God, let her dance again.*

Anger sneaked up on me. Brian should see what she's going through because of him. He should suffer like she's suffering. I gritted my teeth, and my hands balled into fists.

"Has Brian been by to visit you?"

"No." The simple answer held her disappointment.

"What a jerk." He could at least check on her. Someone should bash in his face—

"I won't be dating him anymore."

I took a deep breath and released it. My hands relaxed.

"I don't think he cared about me. Not really. Not like I did about him."

"You don't need him, Jen. There'll be plenty of cute guys to take you out from now on.". *Nicer ones, too*

"Nice ones." Alice caught herself and blushed, but I

was happy she said what I was thinking.

"I appreciate both your support. But just so you know, I forgive him for causing the accident."

I looked down at my lap. "You're a good person, Jen."

Wonderful that she could forgive him. But depending on how this turned out for Jen, it might take me a long, long time.

After we got home from the hospital, I texted Gayle about Jennifer. The phone rang in my hand. David was calling.

"Hey." I closed my bedroom door.

"Hey. That's great news about Jennifer."

"Yeah, it is. I was afraid for a while." I crawled into my bed and rested against the pillows.

"I know." His voice coated and soothed my nerves.

"And I miss being friends with her."

"Of course. How did she look?"

I sucked my tongue from the roof of my mouth. "What a guy thing to ask. She looked pretty bad."

"I figured. But you should be happy she felt good enough to talk."

"I am happy for her, but I'm so angry at Brian. And she isn't. I don't get it. Maybe it's the drugs she's on. I don't know."

"Maybe you'll feel differently after she's out of the hospital and her old self again."

"She'll need a lot of physical therapy to get back to her normal life."

"That's rough. I'm sorry. You sound upset."

"I am. Even if she forgives Brian like she said, I don't. I don't think I ever will."

"You're not gonna let on to Jennifer what you're thinking, are you? That wouldn't help her."

"No." I took a deep breath. "I guess not." Although someone should be angry with Brian.

David lowered his voice. "I promise I'll do everything I can to keep your mind off it."

I giggled. "That's the best idea I've heard all day."

Chapter 15

I'd accumulated so much cash from tutoring, I asked Mom to take me to the bank to open an account.

"Would you like a debit-credit card?" The lady asked me but then looked at Mom. "Because this is a joint account, you both can use it."

Mom's eyes moved around in their sockets as she thought about what the lady said.

"Mom, I'll need it if I buy an airline ticket."

"Right." She told the teller, "Yes, that would be fine."

Everything was falling into place. At the rate I was pulling money in, my goal would be met before summer.

And I hadn't even prayed for the money.

On Friday, Alice and I arrived home from school to screaming and shouting coming from inside the house.

I gripped Alice's arm at the same time she reached for mine.

Those were our parents' voices! I made it to the door a split second before Alice.

Mom and Papa D, with hands clasped to each other's, danced around the kitchen floor on their toes. Their mouths and eyes stretched wide open.

Belle and Chanceaux joined in, twirling and barking from the excitement.

"What's going on?" I dropped my backpack on the floor.

Panting, the adults stopped dancing. Papa D's face was pink to the roots of his hair.

"Did somebody get a job?" Alice draped her book bag on a stool back.

"Yes!" Mom and Papa D answered together.

Mom's face remained flushed as she hugged both us girls.

"Oh, that's wonderful." I hugged Mom.

"Congratulations." Alice kissed Papa D's cheek.

"Wait. Which one of you got a job?" I asked.

"Me," Papa D said. "I start on Monday."

"Yay!" Alice and I shouted.

He held up both hands. "Not as high a position as I had at my previous company, but I can work up to that."

"It's still great." I patted him on the back.

"I'm so happy for you, Dad." Alice hugged him around his middle.

"No more draining the savings account." Mom bent and patted the dogs, but they wouldn't calm down.

"Let's celebrate. Do we have any ice cream?" Papa D slapped the counter with his palms.

As Mom scooped and mounded mint chocolate chip into bowls, Adam got off his bus. He burst through the door to join us.

In the same week, Jennifer had gotten better and Papa D had found a job.

Things would be back to normal very soon. I just knew it.

Chapter 16

"He's here!" Alice pulled back from the window and raced to check her hair in the foyer mirror.

"Alice, chill." I placed the final dinner plate on the dining room table.

She made no effort to play hard to get when it came to my cousin Jerome. But that was okay. As a boyfriend, he'd proven himself to be as sweet and honest and openly affectionate as Alice. Just like he'd always been since he and I crawfished and climbed trees together as kids in Bayou Calmon.

She threw open the front door, and Jerome jumped from his truck. He ran to the porch, took the steps in one leap, and grabbed her. She screeched as he lifted and swung her around in a full circle.

"You're making me dizzy." Her words muffled against his collar, as she buried her face in his neck,

I discreetly withdrew to the kitchen to help Mom with the lasagna preparations.

In a minute, Jerome and Alice appeared.

"Hey, Wendy. Hi, Aunt Cathy." Jerome grinned, his face more bronzy-pink than Alice's.

Alice stayed glued to his side.

I rushed to him and gave him a hug. "It's so good to see you. How are you? Wait—you're taller! And you got a new truck. How's Mattie?"

He chuckled. "Fine … yes, yes … fine. It's great to see you, too."

Mom smiled, a jar of parmesan cheese in hand. "We're happy you could come, Jerome. Is your mom well?"

"Yes, ma'am. She said to tell you hello."

In spite of the divorce between Mom and my real dad, Pete, she was still Aunt Cathy to Jerome and Mattie. She remained on good terms with Dad's sister, Aunt Renee.

Alice opened the refrigerator. "Want something to drink?"

"A coke if you've got it. Thanks."

"Have a seat." Alice popped the top on a can and handed it to him.

He took a sip and sat on a counter stool. "I would've been here sooner, but my mama asked me to stop at Uncle Pete's first. I'm gonna sleep there so I don't have to drive back late at night."

Mom's face didn't twitch or her eyes cloud up anymore at the mention of Dad's name since Papa D came into our lives. "That's understandable. You got here in plenty of time, anyway. We'll have dinner at six."

"My boyfriend, David, isn't here yet." I flinched like a mosquito had bitten me, but I smiled to myself. Had I ever said *boyfriend David* out loud before?

As though I'd summoned him, the doorbell rang and there he was. I opened the door as his dad's car backed out the driveway.

David and I exchanged a brief kiss, and I led him to the kitchen.

"Hello, everybody. Hi, Mrs. Rend." David ran a hand over the back of his hair.

Mom and Alice replied with, "Hi, David."

He offered his right hand to Jerome. "David Griffin."

"Jerome Prejean. Nice to meet ya."

"Cool truck."

"Thanks. Got a deal."

"Sweet."

"Secondhand."

"Looks new."

The guys furthered their discussion using two and three word sentences. How did they do that? Misunderstandings would surely result between two girls—or a girl and a guy.

Alice and I looked at each other. She pursed her lips, eyes twinkling, and I bounced my eyebrows, satisfied our dates had hit it off.

Knowing Alice, she'd make sure this wouldn't be the last time the four of us got together.

After dinner, Alice and I picked up everyone's plates and helped Mom clear the rest of the table. David and Jerome offered, but we waved them away. They were our guests.

Mom rinsed the plates in the sink. "This is your night, girls. Go back to your dates. Adam and Daniel can help me finish."

Jerome, Alice, David, and I sauntered out to the deck

in the backyard. A few mosquitoes caused me to run back inside for matches and a citronella candle. I placed the candle on a short table and lit the wick.

David and I drew two iron patio chairs toward the candle and close to each other. Jerome and Alice did the same.

"Look at the sky." Jerome scooted down in his seat and leaned the back of his head against his chair.

"So many stars, like God created it just for us." Alice leaned back, too.

"The trees get in the way of the sky at my house." Jerome took a deep breath. "The sky seems bigger here."

"It's beautiful. So peaceful." I reached for David's hand and reclined my head.

"Like van Gogh's Starry Night." David caressed my palm with his fingers.

I turned my head and smiled at him in the semi-darkness.

At ten thirty, Jerome sat forward in his chair. "I hate to go, but I still need to drive to Uncle Pete's before curfew." He kissed Alice's hand and stood.

Alice whimpered. "I wish you didn't have to."

"Me too." He pulled Alice to her feet. "I should tell everybody good night."

"They're probably in bed." I stretched my arms high over my head and got up. "We'll tell them for you."

"David, do you need a ride?" Jerome placed an arm around Alice's waist.

"That'd be great, man. I'll text my brother to save him a trip." David typed a quick message.

I sidled up to him, and he brushed his lips against my temple. "I had fun. Hate to see it end."

"So do I." Being without David for more than a day had become almost unbearable. But that wasn't something I should say out loud. Not this early in our relationship.

As couples, the four of us meandered through the gate toward the front yard. Alice and Jerome continued to his truck, while David and I stopped alongside the front porch.

He brushed his lips against my temple again. The tenderness took my breath away. His lips continued along my cheekbone.

I grabbed his shoulders to steady myself.

His lips met mine, soft and easy for a moment. He pulled back.

My eyes must've been huge. Not that he hadn't kissed

me like that before. But an intense warmth consumed me from the roots of my hair to the tips of my toes.

"Is it okay?" He raised his eyebrows slightly.

I nodded, and he kissed me a little harder and a lot longer.

All I could think about was how much I loved him.

Chapter 17

Two weeks before spring break, I refused to take on any more clients no matter how much money they offered me. Lack of planning on their part did not constitute an emergency on my part, and I needed to wind down. I could pick up a couple more clients after the break. As long as I kept adding in all my allowance until summer, I was certain to have enough money for my ticket to Alaska and some for Alice, too.

With relief, I looked forward to having some extra time to run with Alice and Gayle before our first track meet Saturday.

Melissa texted: I'M NOT COMING OVER THIS WEEK.

Even though we had an English paper due? Strange.

Well, maybe some of what I'd taught her had finally sunk in. If she thought she could handle finishing the paper on her own, that worked for me.

Me: THAT'S FINE.

David texted: WILL I SEE YOU AT THE GAME THURSDAY?

Me: I'LL BE THERE.

This was going to be a great week.

By Friday, something was off.

Teachers usually loved me, or at least liked me. I might not have been the brightest star in every class, but I never gave them any trouble. That counted for a lot in public school. But each time I walked into a class, the teacher's posture became rigid. His or her face tightened up like a skunk had wandered into the room.

That went on all day.

"Alice, did you notice anything unusual about the way some of the teachers acted today?" I bent my knee and drew my leg under me to better turn toward her on the bus seat.

She frowned. "No, what do you mean?"

I couldn't really explain it to another person, or maybe I was just too tired, so I shook my head. "It's probably nothing."

Fifteen minutes later I opened the door to my room, and Mom popped into view from behind it.

"Mom!" My heart slung-shot against my breastbone. "You scared me."

She didn't laugh like she normally would've. She squeezed her lips so tightly together that her chin wrinkled. "I received a phone call from your school today, and I'm very disappointed in you." She waited like I was supposed to know why.

I waited in return.

"Some of the teachers suspect you've written papers for their students." She placed her hands on her hips.

My head jerked back. "That's not true! I helped them just like I told you."

"That's not what they claim."

"How could I have time to write papers for fifteen other people?"

"Fifteen?" Mom's jaw hung open.

"Mom, please don't get upset. I can explain to the principal what I've been doing."

"Why would three different teachers tell the principal

that several students' papers sound like they were written by the same person?"

"I don't know. What makes everyone think it was me?"

Mom hung her head and snapped it upward again. "Parents of at least one of the students gave your name."

Melissa! That witch. After I tried so hard to help her, she told her parents? Or maybe it was one of her stupid Stick friends I'd helped. Melissa had made me keep it secret from them, but then she told them herself.

Mom took a deep breath and looked me in the eye. "I want to believe you didn't know you were doing anything wrong, because you've never been in this kind of trouble before."

"I know. I mean, I didn't think I was doing anything wrong. Thanks, Mom."

"But this is big trouble, Wendy. Really big. The principal and the teachers who brought the accusation want to meet with you and me Monday afternoon."

I tried to swallow the dry, fuzzy knot in my throat.

"If it's decided you cheated and helped other students cheat, you'll be suspended from school."

With my knees about to give out from under me, I welcomed the edge of the bed. Suspended? So close to the end of school? I might not be able to finish ninth grade. And what about track?

"Suspended for how long?" I held a hand to my forehead and squeezed.

"I don't know." Mom shook her head. "But I need to look at the steps you and Melissa took—or you and any other student—while working on some of those papers.

Like Jerome had taught me as kids playing on the bayou, I should've trusted my instincts.

David showed up before my track meet Saturday, after telling me he wasn't sure if he could make it.

"Ben said he was ready to see a bunch of girls in shorts, so he drove me. Don't tell Carla." He tugged my ponytail.

He was probably pulling my leg, too, but I wasn't in the mood for jokes.

"Try not to think about what happened yesterday. Focus." He pecked my lips for good luck, and I ran back to my teammates.

Unfortunately, Coach Caisson hadn't been happy with my performance at practice and dropped the bomb on me before the meet started.

"Sit this one out, Wendy."

Whatever. I didn't feel like arguing. With my current frame of mind, I was satisfied to watch Alice in the 400-meter dash and Gayle in the high jump.

David hugged me when the meet ended. "Don't worry. You'll get to run next time."

If there would be a next time.

After dinner, I spread the printed sheets on the floor in my room.

Mom and I examined the evidence carefully. Would it appear I set out to be dishonest in order to make money? Did the stages of work for each student I'd remembered to save prove my innocence? Or my guilt?

"It's going to depend on how they look at it," Mom said. "I believe you didn't set out to do anything wrong, but the other parents are going to want someone to blame. If it isn't you, then their kids will seem like the guilty parties."

"I'm calling Melissa." I got up off the floor, pressure building in my skull. "This is her fault for telling people about the deal I had with her. And after she made me promise not to tell anyone."

"No." Mom's lips pinched into half their normal size. "Passing the blame won't help. If anything, it might hurt you."

Everything that had fallen into place was falling apart. I sat down again and rested my arms on my knees. A full-blown headache had erupted.

"May I have an aspirin?"

Mom placed her hand on my arm and spoke softly. "Who do you know that might have been aware of what you were doing and might be able to vouch for you?"

"Like Alice? And David."

"I don't think they would count. Alice is your sister, and David's your ..."

"Boyfriend?"

Mom nodded.

My eyes must've grown big because Mom said, "What are you thinking?"

"Mr. Stanley."

"Your English teacher from last year?"

"Yeah. I ran into him at the park and talked to him about my tutoring. And he's given me advice through email as I've helped some people."

"Get in touch with him and see if he can meet us at

LeMoyne at three fifteen tomorrow."

Chapter 18

All day Monday, Melissa scuttled out of reach like a crab avoiding a Cajun's net. No wonder she told me she wouldn't see me last week. She'd ratted me out to her parents and teachers, and they, in turn, to the principal.

I filled in details of the whole stinking situation for Alice, Gayle, and David. They acted as a protective shield around me wherever any of them could—in the halls, classrooms, cafeteria, and on the campus grounds.

If it hadn't been for them talking to me, no one would have talked to me at all. As it was, they were the only ones to make direct eye contact, including my teachers.

Why hadn't I trusted my instincts when I first started

helping Melissa? When I had the opportunity to back up and approach my tutoring differently? Why did I take on all those other students when I knew my time was limited?

I couldn't wait for three fifteen to get there. *Please try to make it, Mr. Stanley.*

After the exit bell, Alice caught the bus without me, and Mom arrived in her car as the bus left.

Mom and I met on the front lawn, and she wrapped an arm around my shoulders. "Whatever happens, keep your dignity."

In other words, don't scream, cry, or beg.

We took seats in the waiting area outside the principal's office.

"Mrs. Rend, you and Wendy may go in now."

Mom's eyes widened when we entered the tiny room. She must've thought we'd be alone with the principal like I did.

An uncomfortable silence greeted us, like everyone already there had stopped talking about me as soon as we turned the doorknob.

Melissa's parents sat with their backs straight and chins lifted. Melissa's face was paler than I'd ever seen it. Her haughtiness had evaporated. She shot a sideways glance at me like a cornered bunny expecting to be pounced on.

Three of our school's teachers, two women and one man, clustered on chairs near the principal's desk. The man was our world history teacher. The other two were the ninth grade English teachers.

As if that weren't bad enough, Mr. Stanley was missing.

Mom and I quietly found a pair of chairs next to each other.

Mr. Harrison cleared his throat. "Thank you all for coming. I hope we can shed further light on this disappointing situation that has come to my attention."

The adults shifted in their seats, crossing or uncrossing their legs and arms.

"Cheating is a serious offense, and—"

The door opened with a click, and everyone turned their heads in that direction.

Mr. Stanley walked in, and my heart leapt for joy.

He and Mr. Harrison exchanged nods.

Mr. Stanley took a seat on a small leather sofa farther from Mr. Harrison's desk than the rest of us. He draped his arm along the back.

I took my first deep breath since entering the room.

"As I was saying, cheating is a serious offense,

especially when money changes hands." Mr. Harrison looked around the room at each of us.

The backs of my knees slimed with sweat.

"I've spoken with several of you briefly before now, but I'd like to gather as many additional facts as possible at this meeting. They'll be reviewed over the next few days. A decision will be reached by the end of the week as to who, if anyone, should be suspended. And for how long."

The temperature in the crowded room stifled me. I forced a dry swallow and longed for the bottle of water I'd forgotten in my locker.

One at a time, the teachers presented their information, using the word "student" rather than mentioning any name.

From the way they spoke to Mr. Harrison, it seemed he had already seen the papers in question. A stack of papers sat on the corner of his desk. He listened without comment.

Melissa's mother spoke next. "I discovered Melissa was receiving help when her world history teacher told me her work took a sudden, dramatic turn in improvement. I believe another student approached her with an offer to write papers for her, knowing Melissa could pay well for such a thing."

My breath caught. Melissa's face contorted, and she

stared open-mouthed at her mother.

What a liar! I bit my lip to keep from coming right out and saying it.

She knew Melissa was coming to my house a couple times a week. She picked Melissa up herself every time. Did she think Melissa and I were spending so much time together because we had suddenly become best friends?

Mom's face had turned as white as rice. With jittery hands, she withdrew our papers from an expandable folder. "If I may, I have documentation of Wendy's work progress with Melissa as well as with two other students. These are the papers pertaining to Melissa."

Melissa's mother and father whispered to one another.

Mr. Harrison extended his hand, palm up. Mom handed him the first set of papers.

Everyone was quiet as he spread the papers out in front of him.

"Mr. Stanley, what can you add to any of this?" Mr. Harrison clasped his hands on the edge of his desk.

"I've known Wendy since her days at Bellingrath Junior High." Mr. Stanley brought his arm down from the back of the sofa and crossed his legs. "We ran into each other a few weeks ago, and she told me she was tutoring another student in writing composition. We discussed that briefly, and I offered to answer any questions she might have."

"Did she contact you with any questions?"

"Yes, she emailed me a number of times. From what I could determine, she was teaching like any of us would. She wanted to explain to the students she tutored how to improve their writing. She needed confirmation at times why certain changes should be made. She and I discussed examples of how to improve some sentences and paragraphs."

Mr. Harrison looked down at the papers in front of him, glancing from one to another and back as if searching for what Mr. Stanley described.

Mr. Stanley uncrossed his legs, brought both hands to his knees, and leaned forward. "If Wendy is guilty of doing anything wrong, then I suppose I'm just as guilty for telling her how to make some of the changes she asked me about. And not only in this case. In teaching English, I often give students suggestions to get the effect they desire in a sentence or a paragraph."

He glanced at the trio of teachers. "I believe most of us do. At least those of us who care. I wouldn't be surprised if we sometimes find students' work becoming more similar in style to our own as they imitate us."

One of the English teachers turned toward him and scowled.

I smiled timidly at Mr. Stanley, but his bulldog face remained unemotional.

Mr. Harrison again extended his palm toward Mom. "I'll take those other papers as well."

She passed the rest of the papers to him.

"Mrs. Rend, thank you for coming in. You and Wendy may go."

Mom blinked and opened her mouth as if to say something but closed it again.

"I'll be in touch." Mr. Harrison rose from his chair. "The rest of you, please stay."

Mom and I stood and hurried from the room without anyone else saying a word. We swept past the secretary's desk and into the hall.

Color returned to Mom's face, and she hugged me. "We did fine."

"I should've thanked Mr. Stanley." My limbs were as weak as pine tree saplings, but I held up.

"No, I think we handled ourselves just right." She gave me a weak smile that didn't reach her eyes. "You can thank him later, no matter what the outcome."

I nodded.

"I assume you've talked to Alice about all this?"

"Yes, but what about Papa D?"

"I didn't tell him anything that might've spoiled his first day back to work. Only that you and I had a conference at school. Let me talk to him tonight about what we know at this point."

After Papa D got home from work and had a chance to tell Mom about his day, she led him to their bedroom to tell him about the trouble I was in. At least he'd already started his new job. If I had added to his problems before then, I would've felt even lower than I did.

Their muffled voices seeped through the walls as I passed on my way to Alice's room.

"How stupid am I?" I sat cross-legged on Alice's bed.

"I don't think you're stupid." She perched on the edge and held onto a bedpost.

"Then why am I in trouble?" Deep in my heart the answer came: I'd put my quest for money ahead of what my conscience tried to tell me.

"Things went wrong, that's for sure. Maybe if you'd talked to your mom when Melissa hired you …"

"Yeah, that was my first mistake. Mom pointed that out, though not in those words."

"If I think I should talk to my dad about something and don't, I always wind up regretting it."

I made a growling noise in my throat. "I hate it when parents are right."

Alice chuckled. "Yeah, me too."

The lighter mood flashed and disappeared.

I picked a piece of lint off the comforter. "I'm really scared, Alice. What if I get suspended? I might not finish freshman year with the rest of you. I'd have to go to summer school. And how will that look when I apply for scholarships?"

She chewed her bottom lip for a second and tilted her head. "I have a question. Would you have taken Melissa's money if you didn't think you could help her?"

"Of course not. Although, honestly, my first thought was that she had plenty of it. But I wouldn't have taken her money if I hadn't believed I could actually help her learn. That would've been dishonest."

"I believe you. So what happened?"

"When the work got more time-consuming than I expected, I didn't want to give up the money, so I took a few shortcuts. Actually, a lot of shortcuts. I was selfish, afraid I wouldn't see Mrs. V before—"

"That wasn't a good idea, but I'm not sure it was all that selfish."

"But I didn't care at the time whether you got to go to music camp."

"That's mean, but it doesn't make you a criminal."

"I guess not." I scooted closer to her. "I do care, I mean about you going to camp. Just for the record, when Melissa's friends started coming to me and I knew I could make more money, I thought about how I could help you, too."

"Really? You were going to give me some of your money?"

I nodded.

"Wow, thanks. But I'm on your side, with or without the money. I don't think you deserve to be suspended. I'm praying that the school decides you made a simple mistake."

I jumped off the bed and hugged her neck. "I wish you could be my lawyer."

Chapter 19

"If I invited you to dinner at my house Saturday, would that cheer you up?" David strolled beside me down the hall as we waited until the last second to go to our next classes.

I gave him my full attention. "Yes, I'd love that." Whatever the outcome of the accusations against me, it would be better being with David.

He smiled with his eyes and bit his lower lip.

It took a lot of self-control not to kiss him, but my need for information won out. "Have you heard anyone talking about the potential trouble I'm in?"

"No. Kinda surprised, actually. But no."

I took a deep breath and rolled my shoulders.

Looking forward to dinner with David and his family should make waiting out the next few days for Mr. Harrison's decision more tolerable.

Thursday after school, I paced outside the kitchen while Mom talked on the phone with Mr. Harrison. Finally, she ended her call and noticed me.

I couldn't read her face. "Just tell me. Please."

"You won't be suspended."

I screeched and pumped my fists up and down.

"We had enough paper evidence to prove you worked with students back and forth and your original intention was not to deceive anyone. Mr. Stanley provided more details from your communications with him, so that helped. And you'll be glad to know Melissa admitted to Mr. Harrison that you tried to get her to do all her own revisions, but she refused at times." The lines around her eyes relaxed, but she didn't smile.

"So what's wrong?"

"The teachers are going to make the students involved write new papers, which they should. But you have to pay back all the money you accepted from them as a condition that none of you gets suspended."

"What?" I yelled so loud the dogs fled the kitchen. "That's not fair! If I'm innocent, why should I have to pay it back?"

"Calm down, and look at this as a compromise. You all were involved, and you all get a second chance. Your stepfather and I had already discussed your giving back the money, and we decided it was the best thing for you to do no matter what Mr. Harrison decided about the suspension."

"Why would you do that?" I stomped and huffed.

"Because giving the money back is the right thing to do and the best way to restore your reputation."

"It'll make me look worse." My tears blurred the stripes on Mom's blouse.

"I don't think so. Tomorrow I'll withdraw the money from the bank account and bring it to the school office. Mr. Harrison will call students in one at a time to receive their refund from you. Some of the parents may choose to be there."

My jaw dropped open, but I was too angry to speak.

I buried my face in my bedcovers, screamed, and punched the pillows. Then I threw one across the room, knocking over a little pottery vase Mom had bought for me at a garage sale.

How embarrassing to face all those kids at school to give them back their money! No, it was beyond that. It was degrading!

Didn't Mom and Papa D realize how I'd be pointed out and laughed at? Didn't they care? It would be worse than junior high.

All that work, all that time devoted to earning the money I needed—wasted! I'd never see Mrs. V or Sam again.

I jumped off the bed and cried, pacing the room as tears flowed down my face and neck. With the last of the tears escaping, I leaned against my dresser with both hands.

My sweet little pottery vase lay on its side, cracked. I moaned, tracing the crack with an index finger.

Weak and dehydrated, I guzzled water from a glass on my nightstand, not caring that it was two days old.

My heart was cracked like the vase, never to be the same. And only one person could make me feel better. David.

I blew my nose on the few tissues that remained in

their box and wiped my eyes on the hem of a pillowcase. I selected David's number in my phone contacts. Not that I didn't know it by heart.

He listened quietly while I explained what tomorrow would bring.

"Don't worry. Alice and Gayle and I will do our best to make sure you're not alone during the day. Don't go anywhere by yourself. Wait until one of us can be with you. You have at least one of us in all your classes, right?"

"Yeah." I sniffed. "Thanks. You have a way of making a problem seem like less of one."

"Glad to do it."

All I had to do was get through the next day. I'd be with David at his house for dinner Saturday. Then a whole week of spring break was sure to make everyone forget about my big scandal by the time they returned to school.

I went to the bathroom and pressed a cold wet washcloth to my entire face. Feeling more clear-eyed, I tossed it aside and returned to my room.

Two things in juxtaposition needed to be done: email a sincere thank you to Mr. Stanley and make a list of the dollar amounts to be returned to my ex-clients.

Chapter 20

The big money exchange happened Friday with speed and civility. No one spoke except Mr. Harrison. And then Melissa, who came last, accompanied by her parents.

"Thank you," she said, her voice solemn like I'd bestowed an award on her.

Did I see regret in her eyes? Well, whatever. At least it was all over.

David appeared outside the door to escort me to my locker before leaving for the day.

"Everything's gonna be okay now." He hugged my shoulders and kissed the top of my head.

I nodded. With any luck, someone would get into

spectacular trouble during spring break. Then everyone would have something else to talk about besides my embarrassing payback.

A handful of nonthreatening people remained in the hall, and David left me to catch his brother for the ride home.

Almost out the door to the bus line, and the urge to use the restroom hit. No wonder. I'd been in the principal's office an hour and a half.

I slipped inside.

Good. All quiet.

I entered a stall, and the exterior door to the hall squeaked open.

Great. Who could that be?

Crazy, but I almost drew my feet up off the floor. *You're being ridiculous.*

The girl entered the stall right next to mine. All those empties, and she chose that one?

"Wendy, I wanted to tell you something."

I gasped. Melissa? She was stalking me.

My heartbeat took a second to slow. "Uh, what?"

"I'm sorry."

Sorry? I flushed and left my stall.

She did the same and stood beside me at the sinks. "I

wanted to tell you I was sorry you got into trouble."

I watched her reflection as we both washed our hands.

"I know I was lazy. If I'd done everything you asked me to do with my papers instead of waiting for you to do half of it .... well, I feel bad you had to give the money back."

Her face held a look more honest and friendly than I'd ever seen there. Stunned, I said nothing while I dried my hands.

"And I shouldn't have told my friends what I made you promise not to tell."

I turned and faced her.

She'd admitted everything I'd thought and blamed her for, everything that bugged me so much about the way she'd handled our arrangement. And she'd said she was sorry.

A Stick. Apologizing? Surely that was against the rulebook.

As she stood an arm's length away, vulnerable and searching my face with her near-black eyes, I recognized a human being. Not a Stick, but someone like me. A girl with a conscience.

I wanted to stay mad a little longer, but I couldn't. We both were guilty of straying from the absolute truth. We both could have done better for ourselves and each other.

One deep breath and I exhaled my anger. "I'm sorry, too, Melissa. I could've taken the time and worked with you more if I hadn't gotten greedy."

For the first time since I'd known her, she smiled a genuine smile at me with her glossy pink lips.

David had an out-of-town baseball game that night. I didn't tell him so, but I was relieved to stay home. I planned to veg out in front of the TV in my room most of the evening and think as little as possible. I left the door open in case anyone wanted to join me in those endeavors.

Mom came in and sat next to me. Without saying a word, she gathered a section of my hair from my ear to my shoulder and ran her fingers through it. Just like when I was a little girl in need of comforting.

I turned to her and smiled. She smiled back.

"I love you, Wendy, and I'm proud of you." Mom took my hand in both of hers.

"Thanks, Mom."

A tap sounded. Alice stood in the doorway with a bowl of popcorn.

"I love you, too, Alice. Come on in." Mom bounced off the bed, squeezed Alice's arm, and left the room.

Saturday morning I had a track meet in town. David didn't show, but I didn't expect him because of the game he'd had the night before.

No one I'd helped with a paper, boy or girl, was a member of our team. None of the track and field athletes I knew bothered with that kind of drama anyway when they were about to compete.

We didn't win the meet, but Gayle placed first in the 100-meter dash. Alice placed second in the 400-meter. I placed fourth in the mile. Not what Coach Caisson expected of me. Not what I expected of myself. I was just glad to be able to run.

"Where was your head, Wendy?" Coach raised his arms and slapped them against his thighs.

"I promise I won't disappoint you again, Coach."

The list of people I'd disappointed continued to grow.

Emotionally exhausted and aching in every muscle of my body, I showered. Maybe I should take an afternoon nap. I shot a cool blast in my face and turned off the water.

Better.

Sleep wouldn't matter anyway, because soon the excitement of being with David would rev me up, and all would be well.

I wrung out my hair and wrapped a towel around my body.

The dinner tonight would be a good place for David and me to plan some things to do during spring break. That would get my mind off the past two days. And his parents would be right there to give him the okay.

Due to lack of money, there'd be no trip to the beach for Alice and me, unlike Gayle and her family. That's just how it was. On days I didn't spend with David, Alice and I could get in some extra running, or maybe we could just hang out more and relax.

My phone rang.

"Hi, David. Don't ask about the track meet."

"Oh. Okay. Sorry."

I sighed. "Yeah."

"Hey, did I tell you the dinner tonight is outdoors?"

"No, I don't think so. Like a barbeque?" On my bed, I'd laid out a slim skirt and dressy top, my go-to outfit for a fancy dinner inside. Definitely not stain-proof.

"I'm not sure. Maybe lots of different foods. My parents decided to invite a bunch of people and have a party around the pool."

"Oh." I wasn't ready for David to see me in a swimsuit. And my old one didn't fit anyway.

"Wear something casual in case I decide to throw you in."

"You'd better not!" At least I didn't have to worry about a swimsuit.

"Just kidding. I wouldn't do that. The water's still pretty cold."

"Did you say you're picking me up, or do I need to get one of my parents to drop me off?"

"I'll pick you up when Ben and I get Carla. Is six o'clock okay?"

"That's fine. I'll see you then."

I had three hours to figure out something else to wear.

Chapter 21

Were we headed to a funeral or something?

David sat next to me in the back seat of Ben's car, stone quiet, staring straight ahead. He squeezed my hand until my knuckles ached and I had to pry his fingers off to get my blood circulating again.

And the jaw clenching. The swallowing and blinking. I'd seen dirt fly into his face when he slid into home base, and his mouth and eyes didn't move like that.

I was about to ask what was bothering him when we pulled up in front of Carla's house. She tore out of her front door and into the car in three seconds.

"Hey, everybody." She kissed Ben, seat-belted herself

in, and chattered nonstop as we drove onto the street.

David and I looked at each other, and his small, tight smile was one I'd never seen before.

The Griffin house and backyard were overrun with people, mostly adults. Parents of some of our classmates milled around the pool.

"I'm hungry. Shall we eat?" I started for one of the buffets filled with meats and seafood.

"Let's go to my father's study first." David wore that strange little smile, and his eyes held nothing I could read.

"What's up? I haven't said hello to your parents yet. Is that where they are?"

"They're around." He tugged me by the hand into the house.

Hmm. Maybe the study was the designated make-out center.

We entered a dimly lit, cozy room furnished with a sofa, a desk, and bookshelves. Just what I imagined a lawyer's study would look like.

He closed the door, turned, and faced me. I inhaled scents of leather and lemony furniture polish.

In an instant, he slipped both hands around my waist and drew me to himself with strong forearms.

Surprised by his speed but not the action itself, I melted against him.

His hand moved to the back of my neck, and he kissed my mouth tenderly.

I relaxed and responded to his kiss, his lips warm and soft and minty.

A minute later, he used both hands to gently hold my face as he separated his lips from mine. But he pressed me close, our faces touching cheek to cheek.

My body trembled as I took a few breaths.

"I love you, Wendy," he said, his voice low and hoarse.

I blinked. Did I really hear that, or was I daydreaming? I put a few inches distance between our faces.

His expression, so earnest and sweet, told me I'd heard correctly.

There was no question in my mind what to say. I didn't hesitate.

"I love you, too, David." I smiled, happiness running through veins and arteries, into my bones, and seeping through my pores.

He didn't return the smile but took both my hands,

lowered them, and looked down.

My joy splattered on the floor. "Is something wrong?"

He raised his head and looked me in the eyes. "I wanted to tell you how I feel before I tell you something else."

"What is it?" My empty stomach lurched. I frowned, but come on. Enough with the cryptic talk.

"I have to stop seeing you." His voice croaked.

I yanked my hands out of his. "What? Are you kidding me?"

He swallowed like he'd eaten something spoiled. "I'm sorry. It's my parents. My mom found out you got in trouble at school."

"How did she find out?" Ben?

"It was probably one of the parents helping her with the party who told her. After I got off the phone with you today." His wrinkled forehead sweated.

"But the school decided I wasn't dishonest and I wouldn't get suspended." I backed away to take in the whole length of him.

"I know. I don't understand why they're making such a big deal about it. But maybe that's just an excuse anyway."

"What do you mean?" My hands ran along the sides of

my head as I tried to comprehend the nightmare.

"They said they don't want me dating just one girl."

My voice lowered an octave. "You mean they don't want you dating just me."

He shook his head but only confirmed my statement. "They said we're together too much. They know how I feel about you. I think they'll change their minds later on. They do about a lot of things."

"When?" I fought the tears, my eyes and nose burning for their escape.

His hand stroked my cheek. "Maybe after the summer. If we can get through the summer and start hanging out together again next semester …"

Start all over again for the second time? And after six dates this go-round. Why would our relationship even have a third chance? That didn't make sense.

I shook my head.

"Please try to understand."

He was just whining. A mama's boy. No guts.

"So that's it." I raised my palms in the air. "We can't go out anymore until further notice."

"I'm sorry, Wendy. I really am. I hate this. I really do. But what can I do?" Misery contorted his face. "They made me tell you today."

"How convenient." They either expected I wouldn't cause a scene and embarrass David, or I would cause a scene and give them more ammunition to use against me.

I couldn't hold in my anger. The volcano erupted in a flow of tears, and I screamed like an animal in pain.

He tried to place his arms around me, and I shoved them away with my forearms.

Finally, I hung my head and let him hold me for a few seconds, resting my forehead on his shoulder.

Maybe for the last time.

Without another word, I broke his hold and stalked out of the room. He didn't follow me as I ran through the house to the front yard, grateful to avoid his parents.

I called Mom and told her I had to leave. I waited in the shadows until she picked me up and drove me home.

"Want to talk about it?"

"Later, Mom. Not tonight."

She handed me a new box of tissues.

This was not how I'd dreamed the minutes following David's and my first "I love you" exchange would go.

My life in ruins, I paced my bedroom, twisting the collar of my shirt. Everything had tumbled and fallen, lying on the ground to rot like an abandoned shack on the bayou.

Each time David's last kiss entered my mind, I held

my hands over my ears and screamed inside my head until the memory fled like a startled bird.

Summer would be awful, even more than I'd thought last summer would be, because this awfulness would last all three months.

No David.

No Alaska.

No Mrs. V or Sam.

Not even Jennifer until she—

I stopped and slapped a hand to my mouth.

Sam! He didn't know how things had changed about our plans for Alaska. That I wouldn't see him or Mrs. V after all.

What if I didn't get to see Mrs. V before she died? My heart ached, and I choked back a sob. I might never see either of them again. I had to break the news to Sam somehow. And beg him to try to explain to Mrs. V.

I stepped over to my computer. But now? I'd just had the worst disappointment of my life. Should I bring him down, too? If I did, then I'd feel even worse.

If only Sam and I could speak in person. He'd read my

lips, understand my facial expressions, and see my body language. He'd know how sad and sorry I felt tonight and not just about being unable to see him or Mrs. V. And I could really use one of his hugs.

I forced myself to sit, and I poised my fingers at the keyboard. But I couldn't type the message, because then we'd both feel miserable.

I drew back my fingers.

But maybe it would be better to lump all the misery into one day than spread it out. I should just get it over with.

I stroked the first key.

My email was brief and apologetic. Without revealing too much, I told him Papa D had lost his job and recently had gotten a new one that paid less. I explained I'd tried to earn the money for my ticket to Alaska by tutoring but it didn't work. I asked him to please help Mrs. V hang on until I could get there someday.

Please, God, help me get there.

Sam's reply almost made me cry. Not because he sounded angry or sad, but because the wording was choppy and cautious. "A tough break." "I'm so sorry." "Very disappointing for both of us." That wasn't the way he usually wrote, but more like he tried hard not to make me feel worse by saying the wrong thing.

Too bad it didn't work.

Chapter 22

My breakup with David stung, red and angry and swollen at the start of spring break. My eyes looked the same. The sting reduced to a dull ache by the following day.

It was Alice's birthday, her first with our family, and I wasn't going to let the Griffins ruin it for me. A year ago, Alice and I had hardly known each other, but she'd given me my first book about Vincent van Gogh way before my birthday. She deserved to be treated special.

The aroma of Mom's carrot and zucchini cake with cream cheese icing filled the house, and I followed it to its source.

"It counts as a vegetable this way, so maybe Alice will be able to enjoy more of it." Mom grinned and licked frosting from a rubber spatula as Adam tried without success to blow up a balloon.

Papa D hung paper streamers along the top of the walls, swagging them over windows and doorways. Alice remained in her room, finishing an assignment due after the break.

"Do y'all mind if I give Alice one of her gifts in private?"

Mom and Papa D exchanged a glance. Mom must've read the answer in his eyes.

"We don't mind, honey. Go right ahead."

Alice's bedroom door stood ajar, and I slowly pushed it open the rest of the way.

"Hey, big sister." In one hand behind my back, I carried a small box wrapped in sunny yellow paper.

She laughed and turned in her desk chair. "Yeah, I guess I am, at least for a few more months until your birthday."

I thrust the box toward her. "I want you to have this. Happy Birthday."

Her eyes grew wide and then scrunched up, her eyebrows tilting upward above her nose. "How sweet.

After everything you've been through, you didn't have to get me anything for my birthday."

"It was no trouble. It's something I already had."

She tore off the paper and lifted the lid. Mouth parted, her lips moved as if words wrestled with one another but couldn't make it to her vocal chords.

"Wendy, is this the allowance you saved?" She raised her eyes.

"I think at least one of us should have her dream come true this summer." I walked over and hugged her.

She hugged me back with one arm, the other hand still holding the box. It trembled in her hands, and she lowered it to her lap.

I pulled back. Her eyes had filled with tears. My chin quivered.

"I don't feel right taking this." She replaced the box lid, hiding the cash.

"Why not?" My words came out unintentionally whiny.

"How could I enjoy music camp knowing you're here all summer without Gayle or me and without money to have fun? You'd have to start saving all over again."

"If you don't take this and you miss the deadline to register, you'll be home all summer instead of having fun at music camp. You've looked forward to it for a long time."

"That's not true. I mean, not true that I can't enjoy staying home. It's been so much more fun being part of this family and having you as a sister than it was before."

"So what are you saying? You'd rather stay home?"

She nodded and extended my gift back to me.

"No, I still want you to have it." I held up both palms to block her. "Because we're sisters."

Then the bawling started for both of us.

We would always be in this together.

Regardless of the party preparations, the day seemed quiet without a call or even a text from David. Instead of glancing a hundred times at the screen, I practically took my room apart and cleaned it, just to pass the time.

What would school be like when we had to behave as only friends again? Would Ben watch us if we spent time together and report back to their parents? Would David keep his distance while he and his friends talked about me behind my back?

This breakup wasn't like last time when we'd split up

in anger after only one date. It seemed too late now to go back to being friends. He'd told me he loved me, and I'd told him. So what did that make us?

I sighed and wiped a rag over the frame holding Sam's drawing of Mrs. V and me. Maybe if I stayed in better touch with Sam and talked with him about a possible visit someday, that would help the remaining weeks of school pass quickly.

And I'd stick to Alice and Gayle like glue.

But how should I deal with the teachers? Awkward. Even the ones not directly involved in the paper-for-hire scandal would know about it. Should I act like nothing happened? Like three of them hadn't gone to the principal to complain about me? I really liked my world history teacher, too. Would I be able to look him in the eye? Would he even speak to me?

My computer alerted me of an incoming email. With nothing better to do, I walked over and took a look.

Mr. Stanley!

WENDY:

I THOUGHT YOU'D BE PLEASED TO KNOW I VISITED WITH MRS. PEREZ. SHE REMEMBERS YOU FONDLY AND SAID TO TELL YOU HELLO.

I RECEIVED YOUR KIND THANK YOU. YOU WERE ONE OF

MY BEST STUDENTS, AND I WAS HAPPY TO ADVISE AND DEFEND YOU.

JUST IN CASE YOU'RE WORRIED ABOUT THE REST OF THE SCHOOL YEAR, PLEASE DON'T. ALTHOUGH THE TEACHERS FROM THE MEETING ARE NOT FRIENDS OF MINE, I KNOW SOMETHING YOU CAN DO THAT USUALLY HELPS IN THIS KIND OF SITUATION. IT ALWAYS DOES FOR ME AS A TEACHER. AND THAT IS TO APOLOGIZE AND PROMISE TO BE MORE CONSCIENTIOUS IN THE FUTURE.

THAT GOES A LONG WAY IN RE-ESTABLISHING TRUST.

NOW ENJOY THIS PHOTOGRAPH.

YOUR FRIEND,

EDGAR STANLEY

Mr. Stanley and Mrs. Perez grinned and waved at me in a restaurant selfie.

I smiled. My friend wasn't lonely anymore.

After Alice's birthday party, Mom poked her head into my room. "Daniel and I would like to talk to you for a minute."

"Sure." I raised my eyes from a novel and sat up straighter on my bed.

They entered together. Papa D remained standing, and Mom sat on the edge of the bed near my feet.

"We're so proud of you for giving Alice your allowance for music camp." Mom patted my ankle.

"Thanks. I wanted to. Really. Something good should result from all this mess."

Papa D leaned his back against the wall next to the door and folded his arms across his chest "We know how hard you worked for the other money and understand it was hard for you to give it back."

"It's okay, Papa D. It had to be done. It was the right thing to do."

I turned to Mom. "I'm sorry if the meeting in the principal's office was embarrassing for you."

"Don't worry about it. I have a thick skin." Mom smiled and blinked once, slowly.

"You made a mistake, but that doesn't make you a bad person." Papa D placed a hand on Mom's shoulder.

"I appreciate that. I just wish David's parents felt the same way." I willed the tears to stay back.

"We do, too, honey. Maybe they'll come around eventually." Mom nodded as if she believed it.

I slid off the opposite side of the bed and walked to the window, keeping my back toward them. "I'm worried I'll never see Mrs. V again," I said quietly.

Papa D's deep voice floated smooth and low. "We know that's hard for you to think about. Your mom and I are trying to get the budget fattened back up. If we both have jobs lined up before the end of the summer, we might be able to work something out for you and your mom to go to Alaska for a week."

I spun around, my hope making the room seem brighter.

"Thank you, Papa D!" I ran to him and hugged him tight, smushing my face into his chest.

Mom joined us in the hug.

Sam would be glad to know there was still a chance I'd see him and Mrs. V before the start of tenth grade.

Alone again, I sat at the computer to compose a new message. It shouldn't be worded to get his hopes up too high, though. There was no guarantee there'd be extra funds before the end of summer. But it helped me to latch onto some hope to make the time bearable, and maybe it would for Sam, too.

Chapter 23

Seeing David at school but not being his girlfriend anymore was rough. And my hopes for not being the focus of attention after spring break were dashed. News of our breakup was as hot as cayenne pepper.

When David and I spoke to each other during the day, I only felt worse. Did he?

I willed myself to ignore him, to look the other way if he turned toward me, even in classes we had together. But I couldn't. Once I loved someone, anyone, I couldn't simply cut it off like a faucet.

I'd counted on David all semester to be my protector and cheerleader. What was he now?

If this kind of situation was typical of being in love, I wanted no part of it in the future.

Boom! An exchange of air caused another door in the house to slam shut as Alice burst into my room without knocking. I jolted and spun around in my chair.

"Wendy, you have a priority letter from Alaska." Her eyes held the question that immediately entered my mind. Did something happen to Mrs. V?

She handed me the envelope, and I stood next to my chair, muscles twitching. I had trouble hanging onto the envelope while I tore open the flap.

I unfolded the letter and frowned. What was this?

"What's wrong?" Alice stood at my side.

"This isn't from Sam." I didn't recognize the handwriting.

The message on the first page was brief, so I read it aloud for Alice.

"Dear Wendy:

Your friend has become depressed, and I'm worried she doesn't have much time left. I believe my mother misses you, even in her present condition. Her conversations about you were always cheerful, both in Louisiana and for a time after we moved her here.

Sam told me about the change in your family's circumstances and why you would not be able to visit us at the start of this summer. I hope you don't mind that he shared that information with me.

I wanted to let you know that I appreciate the love and care you showed my mother while you two were neighbors. I know I didn't exactly demonstrate my appreciation when I met you last fall.

Didn't show his appreciation? He was downright antagonistic toward me. And scary.

"So, I'd like to apologize to you now. I would be grateful if you would accept and use the enclosed check to purchase your airline ticket to Anchorage. Please come and try to cheer up your Mrs. V again."

Alice covered her mouth with her hand. I lifted the top page, my heart pounding. Taped to the second one was a check signed by Tony Villaturo.

A puff of air escaped my throat. This was incredible! "Can you believe it, Alice?"

I untaped the check. Alice and I stared at it and then at each other, wide-eyed. We grabbed each other's arms and jumped up and down, screaming.

Mom ran into the room, color drained from her face. "What is it?"

"Mom, look!" I waved the check in the air and held it out to her. "Tony Villaturo is paying for my ticket to go see Mrs. V!"

She snatched the check from my hand and gasped. "Wha—how wonderful! And kind!"

"I know! I thought he hated me." I laughed.

She chuckled. "I told you he was a good person."

Her teeth scraped her lip. "Okay, first things first. You email Sam and let him know you received the check. Thank Tony in the email and ask Sam to forward it to him."

"I will." I grabbed her arm. "So I can definitely go? By myself?"

"Yes!" A grin spread wide across her face. "I still have Tony's phone number, so I'll get him or Sam's mother on the phone and find out when you should be there."

"See? God wanted you to go, and He made it happen." Alice laughed and hugged me. "Another great summer is coming up!"

I'd never grow tired of Alice's complete and never-ending optimism and faith.

Late that night, I received an email from Sam.

WENDY,

I'M SO GLAD YOUR MOM WILL LET YOU COME HERE BY YOURSELF. AWESOME. MY MOM AND SISTER ARE EXCITED TO MEET YOU. LET ME KNOW HOW LONG YOU'LL BE ABLE TO STAY. I'LL LINE UP THE WILDLIFE VOLUNTEER THING.

BUT FIRST LOOK AT THE ATTACHMENTS I SENT IN THIS EMAIL. DAD FOUND SOME THINGS GRANDMA HAD WRITTEN DURING HER LAST FEW YEARS IN LOUISIANA. I SCANNED THEM FOR YOU (IN COLOR, OF COURSE) BECAUSE I THINK YOU'D LIKE TO SEE THEM BEFORE YOU ARRIVE HERE.

Well, yeah. I saved the attachments to my computer desktop and opened the first one.

Wendy and I have become friends. She is so sweet but lonely since her friend Jennifer went away for the summer.

It was all about me! Tears stung my sinuses as I read, and I clutched my t-shirt with a fist. But that wasn't the only thing.

The handwriting. The lined blue paper.

Sam had scanned the pages from a little spiral notebook, the metal spiral showing in some of the scans.

Mrs. V was the writer of the jewelry box note!

My mind raced, trying to add the pieces of the mystery

together so that it made sense. Who could Mrs. V have been arranging to meet at the park after the Mardi Gras parade? And so far in advance? She left Louisiana in September. And did her friend know that she now lived 4,500 miles away?

I racked my brain to come up with someone she would have known that I wasn't aware of. But it was useless to try. The person could be anyone. Someone she met through church or at the hair salon, in the grocery store or at a club meeting.

What should I do first—read all of Mrs. V's writings about me, email Sam back and tell him about the jewelry box and Mrs. V's secret friend, or scan the note I found and show it to him?

My hands trembled, while my vision pulled to her writing on the screen like a magnet to a refrigerator.

All she really has is her mother, who is a wonderful person but a single parent. I'm going to make sure she knows a grandmother's love.

The rest of the pages blurred in front of my eyes, and I wiped the trailing tears with a tissue. She loved me even before I loved her.

I retrieved the jewelry box note from a drawer. Then I found Mom and told her what I'd learned and now suspected about the box. She gave me permission to borrow the jewelry box and photograph it.

With the images of the note and the jewelry box attached, I emailed Sam about my discovery.

In less than ten minutes, I received his response.

THIS IS GRANDMA'S JEWELRY BOX FOR SURE. DAD WONDERED WHAT HAD HAPPENED TO IT. HE REMEMBERS THE CHRISTMAS WHEN GRANDPA GAVE IT TO HER. DAD THINKS SHE GAVE IT AWAY WHEN HER MIND STARTED TO SLIP. HE KNEW HOW MUCH THAT JEWELRY BOX MEANT TO HER, AND SHE WOULDN'T HAVE GOTTEN RID OF IT IF SHE'D BEEN THINKING CLEARLY. SHE MUST HAVE DONE THAT WITH A LOT OF THINGS BEFORE SHE WAS DIAGNOSED WITH ALZHEIMER'S, BECAUSE HE COULDN'T FIND THEM IN HER HOUSE. BUT DON'T WORRY. HE DOESN'T EXPECT YOU TO RETURN THE BOX TO HIM OR TO HER. HE SAID TO TELL YOU THAT HE'S GLAD IT'S IN YOUR FAMILY'S POSSESSION.

I picked up the jewelry box and hugged it, its contents shifting. The box was a part of Mrs. V, imprinted with her personality and the love between her and her husband.

THE LAST PAGES IN GRANDMA'S NOTEBOOK ARE STRANGE, AND I DIDN'T SCAN THEM TO SEND TO YOU. SHE SEEMED TO BE WRITING TO PEOPLE SHE KNEW AT THE TIME, BUT DAD SAID MAYBE SHE THOUGHT SHE WAS

COMMUNICATING WITH MY GRANDPA. OR MAYBE A FRIEND SHE REMEMBERED FROM WHEN SHE WAS A GIRL.

A smile touched my lips. Maybe she was writing to her old friends, my real grandma and my great-uncle she visited in Bayou Calmon.

WHAT DO YOU THINK OF THIS THEORY? MAYBE WHEN SHE WROTE THAT NOTE YOU HAVE, SHE FORGOT WHO IT WAS FOR OR HAD NO ONE TO GIVE IT TO, SO SHE PUT IT IN THE JEWELRY BOX. WE MAY NEVER KNOW. SHE BECAME ANGRY WHEN MY DAD WAS PACKING HER STUFF AND ASKED ABOUT THE BOX AND SOME OF THE OTHER THINGS THAT HAD DISAPPEARED. THAT'S NOT THE PERSON SHE USED TO BE. WELL, YOU KNOW THAT.

I'M GLAD YOUR MOM HAS GRANDMA'S JEWELRY BOX NOW. YOU CAN THINK OF HER WHEN YOU SEE IT.

I'd email Sam in the morning to let him know how much having Mrs. V's jewelry box at my house meant to me.

Poor Tony. He had a lot to handle caring for Mrs. V, but clearly she was in the best place possible. If only I hadn't fought him so hard over taking her to Alaska. But at least he and I could be friends from now on.

I set the jewelry box on my dresser to return to Mom in the morning.

My phone woke me, and I opened my eyes to sunshine streaming through my curtains.

I rolled toward my nightstand and checked the number. "Jen?"

"Hi, Wendy. I'm home from the hospital."

"Oh, I'm so happy." I propped on an elbow. "How do you feel?"

"So-so. But I'm glad to be in my own bed. Can you come see me today?"

"I'd love to. Alice would, too, I'm sure."

"Great! I look a little better than last time you saw me."

"You're always beautiful to me, Jen."

"Aww, thanks. Hey, you won't guess what happened."

Plenty enough had happened—to both of us. "Um, what?"

"Brian apologized to my parents and me."

"Seriously?" The jerk had an ounce of integrity after all.

"And we forgave him. Well, I already had. It took my parents a little longer."

"I'm glad, Jen." If she could forgive him, I guessed I

could do the same. She always was a good influence on me.

"Well, what's been going on with you?"

I opened my mouth to explain but instead burst out laughing. "I think I'd better talk to you about that in person."

After breakfast, I carried the jewelry box back to Mom and Papa D's room and placed it carefully on their dresser.

"I want you to have it." Mom said softly behind me.

I spun around. "Mom. Why?"

She walked toward me. "I love that the box came from you, but you love that it came from Mrs. V. And I'll have more gifts from you, won't I? We have a lifetime for that."

I nodded slowly.

"But you may never have another gift from Mrs. V that would mean as much as this box."

"Thank you, Mom." I kissed her cheek, and we removed her articles from inside the box.

I carried it back to my room and placed it on my dresser. From inside a small cardboard box in my top drawer, I removed the silver puppy charm Mrs. V had given me before she left in September.

It was the first item in my new, old jewelry box.

Chapter 24

The final week of school, David surprised me one morning on the front lawn. "We haven't talked much the past few weeks."

I took a deep breath and hugged my books to my chest. "No, we haven't."

He looked deep into my eyes, his own especially green beneath the leafing trees and clear blue sky. "There's something I want to tell you."

"There's something I want to tell you, too. But you go first." I caught Gayle's attention as she approached from behind David. She turned and headed in another direction.

"If my parents never let me see you again, it doesn't

change how I feel." He looked at the ground for a second and then up at me again, squinting.

"It doesn't change how I feel either. You're one of the best things that's happened in my life so far." Did he want to grab and hold onto me as much as I did him?

"So, what did you want to tell me?" He dropped his book bag from his shoulder.

"I didn't want you to be the last to know that I am going to Alaska this summer."

"I heard."

"Oh."

"How long will you be gone?"

"A month. I'll be a volunteer with Alaska Wildlife Conservation."

"You'll love that. Don't get eaten by a bear." He smiled.

"You joke, but it happens. They won't let teens my age work near the predatory animals, though."

If he was thinking about my being with Sam for a month, he hid it well.

"You've had a good baseball season, haven't you?"

"Yeah. Thanks for noticing."

"I hope you do as well on exams this week."

"Thanks. You too." He reached into his bag.

The brown curls on his head glimmered in the light, and I caught a whiff of his herbal shampoo.

He righted himself, holding a flat rectangular package wrapped in brown paper and tied with string.

"In case we don't get to talk again before you leave, I'd like to give you this." He offered the package to me.

"That's sweet of you." I took it from him, wishing our fingers would touch, but they didn't.

"It's something for the plane, so don't open it until then."

"Okay. Thank you. I'll bring you a souvenir from Alaska."

"Like a prehistoric tooth? That would be cool."

I laughed. "I'll see what I can do."

"Well …" His jaw shifted.

I nodded. "I'll see you."

He gently touched my arm, leaned in, and kissed my cheek. I memorized his smell, his touch, his kiss for always.

Then he walked away.

Chapter 25

I settled into my seat on the plane and strapped myself securely before the airline attendant had a chance to tell me. My new tote bag held Mom's instructions for me, a small thank you gift for Sam's parents, and David's gift.

For weeks in my prayers, I'd asked that David's parents trust me enough someday to let him see me again, other than at school. It was up to God now.

Jen had taken exams with the rest of us and transitioned from her wheel chair. When I returned from Alaska, I'd help her with physical therapy or anything else she needed. Alice would be at music camp for two weeks and would check on Jen before I got back home.

Gayle made me promise to send her a lot of photos. Every day, she said. She wanted to see how brown I'd get from working outdoors all the time. The browner the better, so we'd look more like cousins.

I chuckled and withdrew David's gift from the tote.

The plane wasn't in the air yet, but I was on it, so …

I untied the string and stuffed it into the tote for future use. I untaped the back of the package and removed the brown paper without tearing it. Salvaging and recycling were in my blood.

A book? David had given me a book after saying he loved me? How unromantic. Cold, even. I turned it over to read the cover.

A shiver ran through me, goosebumps rising from my arms to my neck.

David, sweet David. I shook my head. How could you give me the most perfect, most unselfish gift I could imagine?

I squeezed my eyes shut and hugged the title against my chest. *Learning American Sign Language.*

The engines roared, and I was lifted into the sky.

In fourteen hours, I would reach Alaska, but my heart stayed behind on the ground with David.

Questions for Study

1. When is concealing the truth the same or as bad as lying?
2. Is there ever a time when being dishonest is right and necessary?
3. At which point should Wendy have stopped and determined if the way she was earning money was completely honest before she proceeded?
4. At which point should Wendy have discussed her "business" with her parents?
5. Why do you think Wendy was reluctant to discuss her plans or problems with her parents?
6. Which character do you think Wendy should have shown more sympathy toward in the first half of the story? Which one in the second half?
7. What would you have done with the knowledge Wendy gained about Jennifer, her boyfriend, and drinking?
8. What made it hard for Wendy to forgive Brian?
9. Which differences did you see between Wendy and Melissa at the beginning of the story? At the end?
10. How could Wendy have reacted differently when she learned David's news?
11. When you meet someone who is deaf, how do you communicate? Do you know any sign language or would you like to learn?

Resources

Teen Alcoholism:

Addiction Center, Underage Drinking
https://www.addictioncenter.com/teenage-drug-abuse/underage-drinking/

Drug Abuse, Teen Alcohol Abuse
http://drugabuse.com/library/teen-alcohol-abuse/

American Sign Language (ASL):

Signing Savvy, a sign language resource for signs used in the U.S. and Canada
https://www.signingsavvy.com

Handspeak , American Sign Language Dictionary
http://www.handspeak.com/word/

Find a Mentor:

The National Mentoring Partnership, Find a Mentor
http://www.mentoring.org/get-involved/find-a-mentor/#zipsearch2

About the Author
Cynthia T. Toney

Cynthia writes for teens to show them how wonderful, powerful, and valuable they are. Her novels offer hope and humor while addressing issues of concern to teens everywhere.

In her spare time, when she's not cooking Cajun or Italian food, Cynthia grows herbs and makes silk throw pillows. If you make her angry, she will throw one at you. A pillow, not an herb. Well, maybe both.

Cynthia has a passion for rescuing dogs from animal shelters and encourages others to save a life by adopting a shelter pet. She enjoys studying the complex history of the friendly southern U.S. from Georgia to Texas, where she resides with her husband and several canines.

She is a member of American Christian Fiction Writers, Society of Children's Book Writers and Illustrators, Writers on the Storm (Texas), and Catholic Writers Guild.

Visit www.CynthiaTToney.com.

Ways to connect with Cynthia:

Website: http://www.cynthiattoney.com
Blog: http://birdfacewendy.wordpress.com
Facebook Author Page:
www.facebook.com/birdfacewendy
Goodreads: www.goodreads.com/CynthiaTToney
Instagram: @CynthiaTToney
Pinterest: Cynthia T. Toney, YA author
Twitter: @CynthiaTToney

Other Books by Cynthia Toney

"Funny how you can live your days as a clueless little kid, believing you look just fine ... until someone knocks you in the heart with it."

Wendy Robichaud doesn't care one bit about being popular like good-looking classmates Tookie and the Sticks--until Brainiac bully John-Monster schemes against her, and someone leaves anonymous sticky-note messages all over school. Even the best friend she always counted on, Jennifer, is hiding something and pulling away. But the spring program, abandoned puppies, and high school track team tryouts don't leave much time to play detective. And the more Wendy discovers about the people around her, the more there is to learn. When secrets and failed dreams kick off the summer after eighth grade, who will be around to support her as high school starts in the fall?

"Without knowing or caring where I'd wind up, I sneaked out of the house and took off running."

Wendy Robichaud is on schedule to have everything she wants in high school: two loyal best friends, a complete and happy family, and a hunky boyfriend she's had a crush on since eighth grade--until she and Mrs. Villaturo look at old photo albums together. That's when Mrs. V sees her dead husband and hints at a 1960s scandal down in Cajun country. Faster than you can say "crawdad," Wendy digs into the scandal and into trouble. She risks losing boyfriend David by befriending Mrs. V's deaf grandson, alienates stepsister Alice by having a boyfriend in the first place, and upsets her friend Gayle without knowing why.

Will Wendy be able to prevent Mrs. V from being taken thousands of miles away? And will she lose all the friends she's fought so hard to gain?

Newly released from
Write Integrity Press

Someone is determined to finish a murdered hit man's final assignment.

Her father's gone. Her diner's closing. Her car's in the lake. Cat McPherson has nothing left to lose. Except her life. And a madman's bent on taking that away.

Her former boyfriend, Ray Alexander, returns as a hero from his foreign mission, bringing back souvenirs in the form of death-threats. When several attempts are made on Cat's life, she must find a way to trust Ray, the man who broke her heart.

Keeping Cat safe from a fallen cartel leader might prove impossible for Ray, but after seeing his mission destroyed and several godly people killed, he knows better than to ignore the man's threats. Cat's resistance to his protection and the stirring of his long-denied feelings for her complicate his intentions, placing them both in a fight for their lives.

Can she survive when ultimate power wants her dead?

**Thank you
for reading our books!**

**Look for other books
published by**

Write Integrity Press
www.WriteIntegrity.com